The Sunflower
KILLER

DONALIE BELTRAN

THE SUNFLOWER KILLER

Copyright © 2017 Donalie Beltran

ISBN-10: 0-9896362-6-7
ISBN-13: 978-0-9896362-6-1

Available in paperback and eBook

Published by: Killing Time Press, LLC

DEDICATION

This book is dedicated to the three men who have made my life so happy. My two brothers, Lou and Mike, as well as my wonderful husband, Bob.

All three have been so supportive of my love of writing and have not criticized when I came up with some really stupid ideas! Well, okay, maybe a little!

Not everyone has a sister who likes to 'kill people," so when my brothers come to visit, they take my husband's advice and sleep with one eye open. I am not sure why, but I think it's a man thing.

Thanks, guys! I love you all very much!

ACKNOWLEDGMENTS

I would like to thank the Wichita Police Department for their service and the sacrifices they continually make to keep us safe. Although it may not seem like it at times, most of the people you protect are very grateful.

My family and I have the upmost respect for what police officers do and the dangers they face every day. Our prayers go with you.

God bless you all.

I also sincerely thank my beta readers, Walter Danley and Michael Boggia, both excellent writers themselves. Thanks guys, your input was invaluable.

CONTENTS

PAGE

Chapter	1	1
Chapter	2	13
Chapter	3	27
Chapter	4	39
Chapter	5	53
Chapter	6	65
Chapter	7	77
Chapter	8	89
Chapter	9	105
Chapter	10	119
Chapter	11	131
Chapter	12	145
Chapter	13	159
Chapter	14	175

Chapter 15 187

Chapter 16 201

Chapter 17 211

Chapter 18 229

Chapter 19 245

Chapter 20 259

Chapter 21 271

Chapter 22 281

Chapter 23 295

Chapter 24 307

Chapter 25 321

Chapter 26 329

THE SUNFLOWER KILLER

Chapter

1

Just when Detective Roger Duncan didn't think Wednesday morning could get any worse, the captain yelled, "DUNCAN! In my office!"

Good friend and co-worker, Lou McGregor, gave Roger his best sympathy look as he walked to the boss' office.

"Sit." Captain George Parry was not known for wasting words.

He took the chair in front of the desk. The captain didn't like Roger to stand because, at six-foot tall, he made Parry have to crank his neck to look up.

"You look like crap, Duncan." That's Parry. Right to the point.

"Thank you, sir," he retorted. "I didn't get much sleep last night and I'm running low on fuel."

It was the truth. Duncan has a thing for playing chess against his computer. The game is not only relaxing for him, but it's a time when he doesn't think about his current case. For him, that is much needed mental rest.

Unfortunately, time got away from him last night and it was half past two in the morning before he knew it. Yeah, he looked a little rough this morning, but not as bad as he felt inside.

"Well, this should wake you up. I got a call from Chief Randall this morning. Seems our Exploited and Missing Children's Unit is up to their eyeballs in cases. Since you used to work in EMCU, Randall has asked me to give you this case." Parry tossed the file over near the edge of his desk so the detective could pick it up.

Duncan groaned. He left that unit to join Homicide because he couldn't stand to see any more little children abused, raped, or murdered. He just couldn't take anymore. Some of his current cases included a child, but he hated it.

Lord, help me! Can you get me through one more case involving an innocent?

"There is a three-year-old little girl missing from a day care center, uh…Kansas Kidz Center, as of yesterday evening."

"Great. If this is another gang related thing, captain, I swear I am going to take somebody out!"

3

The last homicide case Parry had assigned to him was the death of a nine-year-old Hispanic boy, by gang members getting back at the family of a rival member. That case made him feel like he was right back in EMCU.

It still made him sick to his stomach to think about. He went to the funeral and the site of that child in his tiny coffin was about more than he could handle. Maybe he's getting too old for this job.

But he caught the filth that did it, may they rot in hell. When he arrested the two responsible, it was all he could do not to put a bullet in their ugly heads and save a whole lot of taxpayer's money.

Everybody on the force feels that way from time to time. Some cases just get to a guy. Or a gal. Maybe it's even worse for women. He didn't know.

Of course, we don't pull the trigger, but there is a great sense of satisfaction at the thought of sending the scum straight to hell. Do not pass go, do not collect....

It was during that difficult case, Roger broke up with his then girlfriend, Kristina Peterson. He was not known for long relationships anyway. His co-workers teased him for being a tall, dark, and handsome womanizer.

He actually didn't like the womanizing comments. His inability to stay with one woman very long was due to the fact he had not found the right one. She was out there. He knew it. But so far, he had not found her.

A little boy had been murdered and all Kristina could do was pressure him about the future. She wanted to move in with him and he was not ready for that. Not yet.

Even though he was forty-one, he still felt he would know when the right woman came along. He had been saying that for a lot of years, but he meant it. There had to be something more to marriage than sex.

Marriage is forever. Sure, I liked her. I like her a lot! But 'forever' takes a lot of love. Love I just didn't have for Kristina.

It turned out to be a mutual split. Kristina wanted more than Roger was willing to give. It didn't take long before he heard she was on the arm of another man. *Good for her!*

But no doubt about it, that case changed a lot of things for him. With the loss of that relationship, Roger had not started dating again. It was time to regroup. Maybe he was just getting older, but dating had become more trouble than it was worth. And, well... boring.

The captain brought his thoughts back to the present.

"Take a chill, Roger. This doesn't look gang related, at least not yet. Do you think you can handle this alone? If not...."

"Of course I can handle it alone! I've solved a lot of cases before I had a partner." Duncan was irritated at that question, but then again, his attitude could just be the lack of sleep.

Slow down here, kiddo. Don't get the boss mad. It's a reasonable question.

His partner, Cecil Reynolds, whom everyone called Rocky, took time off to go back to Oregon after the death of his mother from breast cancer. His father is 64 years old, too young to be a widower. However, God never asks permission before removing a loved one.

Roger talked to his partner every couple of days to see how he was doing. It's never easy to lose a parent. He found that out for himself when he lost both his mother and father while going to college to get his law degree.

An attempted robbery ended with both being shot to death. The only thing that kept him in one piece during that time was the fact they died instantly and didn't suffer.

That tragedy also made him change his

major from Law to Psychology, specifically Criminal Psychology. As soon as he graduated, Roger applied at the Police Academy. It became clear to him, he wanted to catch these criminals, not *defend* them!

It was also due to his loss that made Roger graduate from the Academy at the top of his class. His anger and hurt made him study and practice more than anyone else.

No one could beat Roger on the gun range. No one even tried anymore. Give him a gun, any gun, and he would master it. Give him a target, no matter how small, and Roger Duncan could hit it.

He ended up being a bit of a legend at the academy for other students to admire and follow. Roger was even asked to speak to a new class from time to time, to give advice on being the best they could be.

His parents' killer was caught, tried and went to death row. Six years later, Duncan made sure he was there to watch the man die. Only then could he put it behind him.

That was a long time ago, and when all was said and done, it didn't bring his parents back. He missed them every day, but at least that thug wasn't still out there killing someone else's loved ones.

For the case at hand, however, he could handle it alone. Sure, it's nice having another perspective on the clues, but Roger was not concerned.

"How's Rocky doing, anyway? Any word?" Parry was looking at him.

No one knows why he's called Rocky. He just is. It's probably because calling him Rocky was a whole lot better than having to call him Cecil. He smiled at the thought.

Duncan brought him up to date on everything he knew, the funeral, his father's state of mind, and how Rocky was coping. He was staying a while to make sure his father would be able to deal with the loss, plus take care of himself alone.

"Rocky said his father thought a frying pan was a weapon and a vacuum was for cleaning the dog, so he needed to be taught a little bit about taking care of himself!" Duncan and the captain laughed when he passed on the story.

"Okay, the case is yours. Now get out there and find out what is going on. Every moment she's missing.…"

"Yeah, I know. Boy, do I know.…."

And Duncan did know. Kidnapped children usually didn't live long as they quickly outlived their purpose. Whatever that purpose may be.

"Find her, Roger. Just find her." It was obvious some cases were more disturbing than others. They all felt that way. When it involved children, it always fell into the "worst case *ever*" category for any detective.

"On it, boss." Duncan grabbed the file and left the captain's office. Back at his own desk, he opened it and started reading what they knew about the case so far.

A woman, Angelina Jenkins, said her three-year-old daughter, Taylor, was missing from the day care center where she was dropped off yesterday morning. She went to pick her up last night and the center denied her ever having been there.

The preliminary police report from last night was attached. Reading it showed no unusual activity could be found at the day care center. No one saw anyone around who shouldn't be there. No clues at this time. Roger needed to check out the day care center and talk to the mother himself. Firsthand knowledge was the best. The sooner the better.

He left the station, jumped into his black Ford Expedition and headed to the east side of town.

He had no idea this case would change his life forever.

Chapter

2

Within twenty minutes he was at the Kansas Kidz Center. After parking, he did a cursory check of the outside of the building before walking through the front door. It locked behind him.

Duncan was in a completely enclosed glass entry that faced locked glass doors into the building. An arrow showed he had to sign in before he could enter. He was amazed at the security.

Is this for real?

Once he signed and pressed enter on the digital sign-in page, through the interior glass doors he could see the receptionist reading his information. She then came on the intercom and asked what his business was with them. Duncan was stunned!

He showed her his badge through the door and told her he was there about the missing child. Only then did she reach under her desk. A second later a buzzer went off and the two interior glass doors opened. Once inside, the glass doors shut and locked behind him.

He asked for the manager, a Doris McKenzie as he recalled from the file. The receptionist, whose nameplate read Jenny Franklin, picked up the phone, passing on the request.

"Detective, you looking for me?" A woman

appeared from a side door within a minute or two. She was about forty and average size. Graying hair complemented her blue eyes. The worried look on her face told him she already knew why he was there.

"Taylor Jenkins. What do you know about her?"

"I told all of this to the police officers here last night. But, once again I swear to you, detective, I have not seen that little girl. She never came here yesterday. Check my sign-in sheet. No one gets through that door without signing in!" Doris was pale and her hands trembled. Watery eyes showed her to be near tears.

"I saw that. I have to compliment you on your security system. It's unbelievable! If only everyone would have the same kind, especially where children were concerned." Roger had no children of his own, but as a detective, he was impressed.

"Thank you. It really is a necessity when you are dealing with the lives of children. But it wasn't always that way. A year or so ago, we had a little boy's parents go through an ugly divorce. She got custody and he was on strict, supervised visitation due to substance abuse.

"Well, Lester, that was the father's name, came bursting through our front door with a gun and grabbed his son under one arm like a sack of potatoes. He was waving the gun around and yelling that he was leaving with his son and no judge was going to tell him he couldn't. There was no doubt he was drunk as a skunk, or stoned, or both. This only made it worse because there was no talking sense into him.

"Jenny called 911 while I literally fought with him, trying to get him to let go of the child, who was screaming and crying and trying to get down from his father's grasp. Well, after a couple of minutes of struggling, Lester knocked me to the floor and ran out the door with the little boy still screaming under his arm.

"Thank the Lord, the police showed up before he could drive away, but there was a standoff outside. I rushed all of the other children into the back so they would be safe. I also didn't want them to see anyone get hurt. Who knew what was going to happen outside? My employees gave them snacks and read to them to keep them quiet.

"It took two hours before the officers could talk Lester into letting that poor child go. I guess it took that long for him to come down from his high. As soon as he did let his son go, he turned the gun on himself and pulled the trigger.

"I was devastated and scared out of my mind at the same time. The bullet went through his head and into our front window. If children had been playing there…! Needless to say, I was horrified!

"I had to take a second mortgage on my house, but security here became my number one priority. It was quite expensive but worth it. I know these children and my employees are safe now."

Roger responded, "I remember that case. Lester Reisen, I think. He was a real basket case."

"Yes, that was him, detective.

"How's his son these days? Is he okay with what happened?"

"Terry is doing well. He didn't actually see his father kill himself, which is a blessing. One of the police officers had grabbed him up as soon as Lester let go of him. So Terry was looking the other way

"Not only the glass entryway and the electric glass doors that you came through, but even the windows across the front play area are now bullet proof. No bullet will come through that window again.

"Not just Lester, but anyone could have fired

into the center at any time and killed someone. That knowledge came as a shock. There's even a steel back door, to prevent entry that way.

"Some of the parents said it was inconvenient to have to wait outside the front door until someone in front of them signs in, but they all understand the need and appreciate it. I'm grateful for that.

"You probably didn't even notice the eight security cameras, both inside and out, to identify anyone coming or going. I had them hidden so they would not be obvious, but you can rest assured, detective, your presence has been taped.

"We have about twenty-four regular children here, and believe me that is not a huge number. I know the names and faces of every one of them. Every now and then, we get two or three extras for only one day or a week, but we have never had a Taylor Jenkins."

She now looked weak and frail. Duncan was beginning to worry about her.

"Wait. Are you are saying you have *never* seen her, not just that she was not here *yesterday?*"

"That is correct, Detective Duncan. Taylor Jenkins did not come to this center yesterday, nor has she *ever* come to this center. I have checked our records back for the last 4 years—and that is before she was even born! The last three years have been computerized of course, and before that we had handwritten sign-in sheets." Doris looked him right in the eye.

Duncan felt her concerns were quickly becoming his. Not only did he know there was no way anyone could kidnap a child from here but felt strongly she was never here in the first place.

"If rumors get out that a child disappeared from here, I will be out of business, and now I would even lose my home! It's just not true, detective. We love these children and don't let just anyone pick them up. As you saw yourself, if we don't know you, you have to justify your presence or you don't get in.

"We know all of the parents by now, but if a new child starts here, or even comes for one day, we take copies of the parent's drivers licenses so we can identify who can pick the child up. We have strict rules about who can and who can't leave with one of our children. We don't take our jobs lightly, detective." Now she was choking back tears.

"Thank you, Mrs. McKenzie. I have to say I believe you. I will do my best to keep your establishment out of the media as much as possible, but until the investigation is wrapped up, I will need your full cooperation.

"First, I will need a list of every employee you have or have had in the past year, full or part time, their addresses and phone numbers. I also may have more questions, but for now, let's just start with the employees."

She nodded and left the front area for a few

21

minutes while Duncan looked around at the group of children sitting on floor cushions by the front windows, listening to an older woman reading from a story book. Even the older ones were hanging onto every word. It brought back memories that made him smile.

His grandmother used to read to him when he was small. Duncan couldn't remember his grandfather, who died when he was only one year old, but he remembered the hurt he felt when he lost his special Grandma Ava when he was ten.

When Mrs. McKenzie returned she handed him the requested information. She looked a bit more in control, probably due to Duncan supporting her story.

He didn't think Mrs. McKenzie was lying about the child. Angelina obviously didn't sign in with Taylor. The only way he could figure the child disappeared from here, was for it to be an inside job. Never rule out the obvious. This list of employees will be interesting.

He was buzzed out and got into his car. Duncan intended to see the mother, Angelina Jenkins, next. Before leaving the parking lot, his phone rang. The number was 'unavailable.' When he answered, someone hung up.

Boy, that's annoying. Why do people do that?

A little girl was missing from a high-security day care center. How could that happen? Either it didn't, or some center employee was involved.

You couldn't even get into the building without digitally signing in, so an employee would have had to meet them outside the building... maybe promising he would take her in? Anything was possible at this point. But then he remembered the cameras. The two covering the parking lot didn't show a Taylor Jenkins, and neither did the two at the front door.

So the mother had to have lied about

dropping her off. The next question is 'why?'

He recalled a case he had heard about in Missouri somewhere. A woman got tired of her five-year old kid and killed him. To cover him being gone, she claimed she took him to a local day care center. It was pretty much a "she said, they said" because the center didn't have cameras to prove or disprove the mother.

The mother threatened to sue the center for 'every dime they had' for allowing her child to be kidnapped from their property.

She would have gotten away with it if they hadn't found the child's body stuffed under the mother's back porch. The woman wanted to be free of the son and have a big payday for her drugs. She was convicted on the charge of murder one.

Could this be something that horrible? Did this woman read about that case and felt she could make it work? You never know anymore.

Evil is everywhere, God. Why do you allow people like that to have children? Please, don't let this innocent child be dead.

He went over everything in his mind as he drove to the southeast side of the city. It took a good fifteen minutes to maneuver the busy streets from the day care center.

Roger pulled into a low-income area apartment complex off East Lincoln St. They were all very small, ground floor apartments, about four to a building.

He had no idea what kind of mother he would be talking to. An alcoholic, druggie, or maybe another woman who didn't like her whiny kid.

He didn't know for sure, but as much as he dreaded it, he was about to find out.

Chapter

3

When he knocked on the apartment door, it remained quiet for a couple of minutes. He started to knock again when the door opened slowly. That's when he saw her.

Angelina Jenkins was a small woman, no more than five-foot-two, and slender. Too slender actually.

"Angelina Jenkins?"

She looked gaunt, but nodded and moved slowly out of the way so he could enter.

Roger couldn't help but notice she was beautiful. The scarf around her bare head bore the obvious news of chemotherapy. Angelina looked ill and exhausted, but her hazel eyes were still bright. Well, so much for the idea of a killer mom.

She pointed to a chair, where he sat down. The end table next to him had three small framed pictures. Two were of Angelina in better days. One showed her when she was a gorgeous pregnant lady with a smiling man standing by her side. Another was with a beautiful blonde haired little baby with the most incredible sapphire colored eyes, that he had to assume was Taylor. The third was the child alone. He couldn't take his eyes off of that one.

"Yes, she is a beauty, isn't she? Taylor got her looks from my side of the family and her father's coloring. He had blonde hair and those awesome blue eyes." Her eyes were at half-mast, but her smile still came through.

Angelina's remark brought him back to the present. She was now settled on the couch.

"Yes, she certainly is a pretty thing." Duncan felt an intense anger that she was missing, maybe scared or hurting somewhere. But then he was on the job and had to get the information he came for.

"I am sorry to bother you with this, Mrs. Jenkins, but I am Detective Roger Duncan with the Wichita Police Department. I am going to need a picture of her, and I will need to ask you some questions."

"Angelina, please. Not a bother, detective. Yes, you can take that one out of the frame. It was taken only four months ago. You must find my Taylor, detective." Angelina's voice was hardly more than a whisper.

After removing the picture, he put it in his

suit pocket and continued with the question he hated to ask, "Okay, tell me when you dropped off…uh, Taylor, at the center yesterday morning."

"Oh, I didn't, detective. I have never taken my child to any day care facility. My sister did that–without my knowledge. Adriana. Adriana Mason. I have to tell you, she's my identical twin sister. But don't let the 'identical' part fool you. We are thirty-two years old and look alike, or at least we used to before the chemo, but we are as different inside as two people can be."

Her eyes held sadness as they teared. Roger wanted to reach out to her but knew he couldn't.

"You see," she went on, "I have had chemo once a month in an attempt to stave off the obvious. It apparently didn't work, but one has to try, don't they? At least I don't have to go through it anymore." She gave a doleful smile at the thought.

"My sister is the only family I have left so I

called her day before yesterday, on Monday, and asked her to pick up Taylor yesterday morning and take care of her while I go to the hospital for chemo. She said she would."

"You asked her two days ago? What about last month or times before that?" He had to move in closer to hear her speak. She spoke softly, and some words came out with a rasp.

"My neighbor, Annie—Annette Gleason— would watch her, but she passed away two weeks ago. She was only 69 years of age. Sweet lady and a dear friend. I really miss her.

"I don't know any of my other neighbors, so I had no choice but call Adriana. So that you can get a true picture here, Detective Duncan, my sister and I are not close. That whole 'twins think alike' thing didn't happen for us.

"She has always been the ambitious one, while I was not. We both went to college, but since I loved children, I became a school teacher. At least I was until I got sick.

"She went to law school and become an attorney. My whole goal in life was to be happily married to a nice man and have a family. Adriana wanted to be CEO of a billion-dollar company!" She smiled at her remark.

"However, she settled for being a lawyer. I guess she is doing really well because she showed up in a beautiful pink suit with several pieces of diamond jewelry. I did see she left in a silver Mercedes. But I never had the chance to ask her anything about her life."

Glancing at another picture of Taylor, Angelina broke down in tears again. Roger's felt sorry for her pain. A few minutes later, she composed herself.

"I got what I wanted in life as well, at least for a while. I fell in love and married Kenneth Jenkins, a wonderful man who loved me back. Ken was an accountant and with both our incomes, we lived a nice middle-class life. At least nice to us. Middle-class is certainly not

Adriana's idea of nice.

"My dear husband died in a car accident two years ago when a drunk driver ran a red light and broadsided him. They told me he died instantly. Taylor was just a baby then, but it seems like only yesterday. So, it has been only the two of us since.

"Adriana would never come around here unless she absolutely had to. She hates 'poor people.' Oh, I see your smile, detective, but I'm serious. She looks at me in complete disgust. Please don't get me wrong, it doesn't hurt my feelings that she feels that way. I don't care a bit. Adriana is…well, Adriana. I just don't see the world as she does.

"When I came down with cervical cancer six months after Ken died, I called her and left a message telling her I had a life threatening disease, but she never even called back. She really couldn't have cared less. What happens to me, or anyone else for that matter, is just not a concern of hers.

"Since I couldn't work anymore, I went on disability and we had to leave our home for something… cheaper. Luckily Taylor is so young that she hasn't even noticed the difference." Angelina's sad face told volumes.

"Forgive my rambling, detective, but back to your question, Adriana picked Taylor up yesterday morning right on time and I got ready to go to the hospital. I didn't know until later in the morning that she had taken her to Kansas Kidz Center. She called me to tell me that was where I was supposed to pick her up. I was very upset that Taylor was with strangers, but there was nothing I could do about it then. My sister obviously had no intentions of taking time off from her precious work for her only niece.

"Oh, I told you I love children? Well, Adriana hates children. Did I mention that?" Angelina tried to smile. "They take up her precious time and money. That is absolutely not allowed in her world."

Her shoulders were now slumped, making her appear weaker. He knew he needed to leave so she could rest.

"Ma'am, uh, Angelina, I will need her address and phone number, if you don't mind." That was all Duncan could think to ask at this time. He had thought of several scenarios on the way over here, but nothing had prepared him for Angelina and her circumstances.

This whole story was sad, if not downright depressing. He has worked dozens of cases and some would get emotional, but this one was different. He couldn't put his finger on it, but it was definitely different. He could feel it in his gut.

This woman, however, didn't seem to mind that her only relative didn't care about her or that she was dying. Well, I guess when you have terminal cancer, everything else doesn't seem to be important anymore.

"I don't know where she lives, but I have her private work number. She gave that to me years ago when I had the audacity to call her office and leave a message. She called me back with her private number and told me not to call the office number again. I guess she didn't want to be associated with a woman married to an accountant."

She wrote the number down and handed him the paper. Angelina then looked him in the eyes. "I am told I only have a couple of months to live, detective. I want my Taylor to spend that time with me. Find her. I can't stand this pain in my heart. Find my baby, detective."

He nodded and left.

Duncan had limited information, but that will have to do. While leaving Angelina's area, he called the number and got Adriana's personal voice mail and left a message for her to call him back immediately. He didn't know when she would pick up her messages so he headed back to the station.

One thing he did know. He had never met her, but he knew without a doubt, he didn't like Adriana Mason very much. No, not much at all.

~~~

The conversation with Angelina was one of his toughest in a long time and weighed on his mind. She knew she was dying and so did he. Having to deal with a deadly disease, the debilitating side effects caused by chemo, and then have your only child vanish, is more than anyone should have to bear. Roger's heart went out to her.

Please, Lord, let me find Taylor alive.

At his desk, he made the copious notes he was known for, careful not to exclude any comment or impression. It may be important later. Now and then, Duncan would take Taylor's picture out of his pocket to look at it.

It seemed like she was staring right into his heart. He knew this case was getting personal to him, but he wasn't able to stop it. When he thought about it, Roger wasn't even sure he cared.

Late that afternoon, he called it quits and went home. The lack of sleep and mental exhaustion was getting to him.

That evening he went to bed early without a thought of playing computer chess but had to fight nightmares most of the night.

A beautiful little girl was in terrible danger.

Chapter

4

The next day, Duncan had not heard back from Adriana Mason. Remembering how she treated her own sister, he wasn't going to be on the receiving end of her apparent superior attitude. Plus, he was anxious to know about her time with Taylor.

Checking her background didn't take long. She was a criminal defense attorney for the firm Mason & Porter, LLC, here in downtown

Wichita. She owned an expensive home and car. Her partner's name was Derrick Porter, a criminal defense attorney, who also had a high-end home and car. Rumor has it, he was her boyfriend.

He remembered something about that name and looked deeper into Porter. Seems he made news in the Wichita Eagle newspaper last year when he got into trouble for possible jury tampering on a trial in which he was the defense attorney.

The article said 'possible' only because they thought he had done it, but couldn't prove it. He got a slap on the wrist instead of being disbarred. He continued to deny it, of course.

The whole incident turned honest people away from hiring him, but it brought in every felon in town to be his clients. It was obvious why.

If I were a felon, I would certainly want an attorney who could get to the jury so I would get off scott free! That's a no-brainer!

Yes, the firm seemed to be thriving and their fees were high. From what he had learned from Angelina, that is exactly what her sister wanted.

Because of Mason's silent treatment, Duncan decided to pay an unannounced visit to her office that afternoon.

About fifteen minutes later, he pulled into the parking garage of the downtown office building that held her law firm. He took the elevator to the firm's floor.

Upon entering the office, he went up to the pretty, black receptionist Stephanie Weathers, whose name appeared on the brass desk sign. He asked to see Adriana Mason.

Oddly enough, the woman did not call her boss on the phone. Instead she went through a door to the back offices. Duncan waited for another few minutes.

When Stephanie returned, she appeared flustered and said Ms. Mason couldn't be disturbed at this time and if he could come back some other time?

Duncan's skin did a slow crawl. Typical of some arrogant attorney. She thinks she is above the law, just because she *knows* the law. What that woman was not taking into consideration was that he *also* knew the law, and at this very moment, he *was* the law!

He leaned down on the reception desk, smiled and said in a quiet voice, "Stephanie, is she in a meeting with a client?"

"No."

"Is she perhaps on the phone?"

"No."

"Then go back in there and tell her she has ten seconds to appear up front or I will take her out of here in handcuffs, and we will talk down at the station. Okay?"

Stephanie got back up and said, "Okay!" She smiled as she went back through the door.

About half a moment later, Adriana Mason appeared in the reception room. The first thing you noticed about this woman is she gave beauty a new name. Long, deep brown hair and hazel eyes. Yes, Angelina would have looked just like her if she hadn't gotten sick.

This version wore an expensive low-cut lavender dress and matching stiletto heels, making her appear much taller than her sister. There was no doubt she wanted to appeal to the male population. Duncan struggled not to show his appreciation but doubted it worked. He decided to play nice.

"Good afternoon, Ms. Mason. I am glad you could make some time for me today." Duncan poured the sweetness all over her.

"Of course, I would always make time for a

detective as handsome as you are. But we don't need to do this here. Let's go get a cup of coffee." She headed for the door, so Duncan followed.

About a half block away was a fancy restaurant that he had to admit was just another one he had never been to. That list was long because he didn't have a need to rub elbows with the rich.

After they were seated and served coffee, he decided it was his turn to take over.

"Ms. Mason, I need to talk to you about yesterday morning."

She remained quiet and stared at him.

Just as he was about to go on, he heard someone call his name.

"Roger! What a surprise to see you here! We were just on our way out." It was Kristina, his old girlfriend. She looked happy and was on the arm of a man who was well dressed.

"Kristina! What a pleasant surprise. Nice to see you again. This is...." Before he could finish, Adriana took over.

"I am Adriana Mason. Attorney Adriana Mason. It is always a pleasure to meet a friend of Rogers." Adriana was dripping sugar.

"This is my friend, Doctor Mark Weston. Mark, this is an old friend, Wichita Police detective, Roger Duncan." Kristina quietly ignored the obviously superior attitude of the attorney.

Roger stood and they shook hands. It was apparent the good doctor and Kristina were close. Goodbyes were said by all, then Kristina and the doctor left.

"You impress me, detective. I didn't know you associated with the upper crust. Maybe we should get to know each other better." The sexy look was not lost on Roger.

He ignored the comment. His ex-girlfriend had more class than this woman ever would. Give me the Kristina's any day! He returned to the reason he was there.

"I understand you took Taylor Jenkins to the Kansas Kidz Center yesterday morning. Is that right?" Duncan did his best to be polite, but it wasn't easy.

"Of course that is right. I told Angelina I did. I can't believe what is happening! How can they say they haven't seen her? I am so worried, but I can't think of one thing I can do."

"Why do you think the center is saying they never saw the child?"

"I have no idea. I am so upset. I know my sister must be, too. Obviously someone took her away from there! You should be questioning them." Her worried face stared at Duncan.

Then he changed tactics. It was time to be on her side.

46

"Well, it *is* possible someone stole her from there. I mean, I was there yesterday, and no one even notices when someone comes through the door. I was there several minutes before anyone asked me what I wanted. There were kids running all over the place. They looked unsupervised to me!"

"Exactly! Those were my thoughts, too! It's like they just didn't care I was there with a kid! I mean, time is money to me." Adriana's dramatic response was just what he wanted to hear. Her own words proved she had never been there.

"Sure. I can certainly see your point. Would you please describe your movements of yesterday morning for me, up to the time you dropped her off."

"Well, I picked the kid, uh, Taylor, up over in that sleaze bag apartment complex my sister lives in. There ought to be a law against such places. I wish she would move somewhere more respectable, but we all can't have money, right?

"Anyway, then I went to Martha's Corner Coffee Shop in Delano, just a couple of minutes from here, actually. I go there every morning of the week, even weekends. It isn't very convenient on the days that I don't work, I have to admit, but they have the best lattes so it is worth the drive. I live in Eastborough as you probably already know.

"So, I got... uh, Taylor a donut and then drove her to the center. Like I said, I had to wait to even get their attention, but they did finally take her in. I made it back downtown on time.

"I know my sister wanted me to take the day off to watch her, but I knew I had a packed schedule. You can't disappoint the clients, now can you? But, now I wish I had. This is terrible!"

Duncan had to admit Adriana was good. Really good. If he had not known better, he would have believed her every word. She must be dynamite in the courtroom with the jury. Some people were just born actors. The truth doesn't matter, just say what you want them to hear.

Duncan knew he wasn't going to get any more out of this woman right now. If he did, it would be more lies. She didn't seem to have any problems flirting with a man, even a police detective. But then again, men made up the majority of most juries, don't they?

Time to play *his* 'flirt' card.

"Well, I must say, I was not expecting you to be so...uh, beautiful, Ms. Mason! Do you mind if I take your picture? The guys back at the station aren't going to believe what I tell them if I don't have proof!" Duncan's big white smile always worked.

Obviously pleased by the compliment, she stood by the table and posed for him like a star on the red carpet. He steadied his Samsung Galaxy cell phone, snapped the picture and thanked her profusely.

"Can I go back to work now? I am up to my ears.... " She stuck out her lower lip in a brief pout.

He had obtained the information he came for. It was time to leave.

"Okay, get back to work. But first, I will need a list of all your employees. Names, addresses, phone numbers, the works. You don't mind, do you?"

She smiled and called her receptionist on her cell and instructed her to email the info to Duncan. It took a moment before she was able to get his email address straight, but it finally worked.

She grabbed her purse to leave.

"Don't leave town, now." Duncan gave her another big smile. He heard her sweetly say as she disappeared through the door, "Bye, now…, come see me any time."

He went to the front to pay the bill and found it had been put on Adriana's tab. Seems she had insisted.

Chapter

5

After he left the restaurant, he went back to the police station almost certain that last encounter was going to make him physically ill. The receptionist had emailed the info he needed and now he needed time to go over each one.

Of course he knew Adriana lied about taking Taylor to the center. For whatever reason, she was involved with Taylor's disappearance. Her own niece. She had to be one of the most hardhearted people he had ever met.

The next couple of hours were spent making notes and going over the information he had. He did background checks on all of the employees of the law firm, to add to those who worked for the day care center. No one stood out.

When there was nothing more he could do, he called it a day. Heading home that evening, that little girl's picture stayed in his mind.

Dear God, please don't let that child be at the hands of a sexual predator. She has been kidnapped by someone, I know. That's bad enough, but not for sex, God. She is only three years old. Please.

That's all Duncan could think it was. It certainly wasn't for ransom, because there wasn't anything to get. Angelina had nothing left to give.

Why would anyone want a three-year-old? He choked just thinking about it. What ends would Adriana go to in order to pad her bank account? He almost didn't want to know.

To keep the demons at bay, he stayed up and played chess on his computer.

He turned off his phone after he received two calls, and the person hung up when he answered.

When Duncan did make it to bed, he was awakened twice with nightmares that brought horrible pictures of what might be happening to Taylor. Once, he even had tears in his eyes.

~~~

Early Thursday morning he called to check in with Captain Parry and told him he was headed to the Delano coffee shop.

At seven in the morning, he went outside to get into his car and was shocked to see his windshield smashed in.

Now what? Did a gang member find out where he lived and wanted to get back for the child killers he put in jail? He recalled the hang-ups from the night before. This did not bode well.

He called the captain again and explained his situation. A patrol car was sent as well as a crime-scene investigator. Everything was dusted for prints, including the rock that smashed through onto the seat, but none were found.

After forty-five minutes, Roger could allow the new windshield to be installed. The repair van had been waiting at the curb until the cops were through with the vehicle. He gave him a tip for his trouble.

Roger was going to have to pay better attention to what was going on around him. One thing is for sure, he would be putting his car into his garage from now on. The captain thought he should have a patrol car watch his house at night, but Roger declined. At least not yet.

It was ten that morning by the time he made it to Martha's Corner Coffee Shop in Delano. A tiny town swallowed by Wichita many years ago, had a few businesses still using the name. Delano was to the west of downtown Wichita, only minutes away from the station.

Roger Duncan parked across the street and walked over to the shop. Once inside, he got into the short line waiting to be served. Some patrons sat at tables to chat with each other. But most that came here were already on the job somewhere by this hour.

He wanted to arrive early to talk to the woman who was working the morning Adriana said she came in with Taylor. Roger hoped the same person was still on the job.

It only took a few minutes to get up front and he spoke with a girl whose name tag declared her to be Linda Copely.

"Linda, I am Detective Roger Duncan with the WPD. Were you working two mornings ago, on Tuesday?"

"Yes, I always open."

The tall girl with the spiky tri-colored hair was friendly. She told him she was the opening barista at the coffee shop, and had been for seven years, and worked until noon. When he showed her Adriana's picture, she recognized it right away.

"Oh, yeah. Adriana Mason. She comes in here every morning, whether I like it or not." Linda smiled.

"Okay," Duncan said, smiling back, "Tell me why you feel that way."

"Why do I feel this way... let's see... Well, Adriana is a self-centered, egotistical brat who thinks the world is her plantation and everyone in it is her slave. That's why I feel that way!" She laughed out loud.

"Well, I think that pretty well sums it up.

But, what do you *really* think?" They both laughed at his silly joke.

Duncan asked if he could get a regular cup of coffee and maybe she could join him at a table for a few moments since all patrons had been served and had left or seemed to be happy at their tables. She agreed.

After they both got comfortable and Duncan was enjoying his coffee, he asked her if Adriana was alone on the morning in question.

"NO! Sorry, didn't mean to yell. I mean, I have *never* seen her with anyone except her boyfriend, Derrick what's-his-name, the crooked attorney. Boy, do they ever make a pair. But most of the time she is alone.

"Anyway, she had a little girl with her. I couldn't believe it. Adriana hates children. I have heard her say nasty things about children several times over the past couple of years. And I wasn't eavesdropping, either. That woman *wants* everyone to hear her opinions.

"You wouldn't believe this child. She was beautiful. Blonde hair with these incredible blue eyes. Like sapphires, really!"

Duncan pulled out the picture of Taylor and Linda identified her as the child with Adriana. He then asked for a word by word accounting of what Adriana said and did.

"Okay, well, let me think. She was in line. When she got up front, I said *'What'll it be today, Adriana?'*

"She snapped back at me, 'That's Ms. Mason to you if you want to keep your stupid job. I'll have my usual. ' She was leaning up on her tip toes, if that's possible in stilettos, looking over the counter at the donuts. She then ordered one 'for my... uh, my small friend.'

"Well, I looked past the pressed pink suit and my jaw dropped: *A little girl. With Adriana?*

"The smiling girl looked to be about two or three. She looked happy enough, even though

Adriana continued scolding her for touching things and getting her "sticky fingers all over everything in the store.

"She said, 'This is Taylor,' while stuffing a too-large piece of donut in the girl's mouth. I was scared that child was going to choke, but she somehow took it in stride. 'I'm just watching her for a bit, while my sister has chemo.'

"Oh! That's... sweet," I fibbed. There was nothing "sweet" about seeing Adriana Mason with a young child. *God help that little one,* I thought at the time.

"When Adriana left, she struggled to juggle her latte, the door, the child and her cell phone. But she managed to leave.

"What surprised me was the fact she turned right, outside the door and disappeared around the right side of the building, with the little girl, instead of crossing the street where she usually parks. Anyway, I returned my attention to nicer customers and carried on.

"About ten minutes or so later, the line was gone and I'm sipping on my own cup of latte when I see her come back from the right side of the building. She crossed the street, got into a Mercedes and drove away. That little girl was not with her. She was not there.

"At the time, I figured the sister must have met with her around here somewhere and picked her child up. Maybe the sister lived around here. I didn't know.

"That's it, Detective Duncan. Oh, and yes, she was here this morning, but she was alone. She never even spoke to me, except to say 'usual.' I have to admit, that was the best part of her being here."

For the next thirty minutes, Roger Duncan and Linda went over each item to make sure he got them right. He then thanked her and left.

Back at the station, he told Captain Parry what he found out from the coffee shop. Both knew it was time to take a close look at Adriana

Mason.

She had become suspect number one.

Chapter

6

The next day was Saturday and Detective Duncan spent it at the station. He had interviews with the day care employees to sit through.

He rechecked all of the information he had gathered. Background checks were piled high on his desk. Over the last two days, they had multiplied until he could no longer ignore them.

He knew Adriana Mason was responsible for Taylor's disappearance, but he had to get his ducks in a row. You can't arrest an attorney without proof and preferably witnesses. Lawsuits would bury them for the next ten years, to say nothing of ruining his perfectly good career.

He could just hear her defense attorney now.

"Ladies and gentlemen of the Jury, the State has insufficient proof. They have the word of one witness. Surely we are to believe an educated woman like Ms. Mason over a barista!"

"Ladies and gentlemen of the Jury, the prosecution has not submitted one reason why Ms. Mason would do such a thing to her sister, her identical twin sister!"

"Ladies and gentlemen of the Jury, my client didn't need to sell her niece. She is very wealthy in her own right. What would she have to gain? You must find her innocent of all charges!"

Duncan needed answers to those questions.

He knew Angelina would probably not be around by the time it went to trial, so even her word that Adriana picked up the child could be made suspect.

"Ladies and gentlemen of the Jury, the mother was undergoing chemotherapy treatments. She was hallucinating when she thought her sister picked the child up. It didn't happen. Who this sick woman entrusted her child to, we will never know!"

He was exasperated. If Adriana was responsible for what happened to Taylor, and he knew she was, he wanted her to pay dearly. This had to be done right. The first time.

Duncan had a couple of beat cops check the area on all sides of the coffee shop for security cameras. Maybe he could find out what she did with Taylor.

Waiting for their report, the one thing that bugged him the most was "why." Why was she missing? Who would want her gone? Was it just for money or was there another reason lingering somewhere he couldn't reach?

Did Adriana hate her sister enough that she wanted to hurt her? But again, why? Angelina was already dying, what purpose was there?

Over and over, the same questions. Unanswered questions are a bane to a detective. Their whole purpose for being is to have answers. Roger Duncan had none.

Just before his first interview, the police officer called to say there were no security cameras in that area. He couldn't believe it. Nothing was working in his favor.

First to arrive was one of the main caregivers, Blanche Nelson. She was the one he saw reading to the children.

"I'm a widow, you know, so I have the time to work part time. I love children, so the day care is perfect for me. I am appalled about the missing child, but I assure you, detective, I was there when all of the children arrived and she was not one of them. No sir, she was not one of them."

The second caregiver, Kathy Morgan, was next.

"I had the day off when the little girl went missing, but the thought that anyone would kidnap a child is repulsive. You have to find them, detective, and make sure they never get near a child again."

There were two assistants to the older ladies. They would help with snacks, lunch and nap time. They also picked up the toys and put them away at the end of the day.

The first was Charity Banes, a young woman of twenty-two.

"Mrs. McKenzie is wonderful to work for. She loves those kids and wants what is best. We keep that place neat and clean. With twenty-some kids, sometimes that is a challenge, but we get it done.

"No. I have never seen that child…Taylor is it? A beauty like that you would remember, wouldn't you?"

The second was Berry Underwood, a boy in his late teens.

"The kids are neat. I have fun playing with them and helping them with lunch. I mean, you have to love kids to work there, know what I mean? Mrs. McKenzie is cool but she doesn't put up with no playing around. Those kids are number one. She really cares that they have a fun time while they are there. She is always buying new toys for them.

"No, I never saw the kid in the picture. Sure is a pretty little thing, though, isn't she?"

The last interview was with the night janitor, a black man by the name of Lester Calvin.

"I'm there at night. I don't know any of the

kids or nothing. I just clean up, you know, mop the floors and stuff. Yes, I have a key to the steel door out back. Gotta get in somehow. No, I have never been through the front door.

"No, I ain't never give out no key to anyone else. Think I want to lose my job?"

Duncan was getting discouraged. There wasn't anything out of the ordinary. He felt like he was back where he started.

When am I going to get a break here, Lord? Something? Anything?

He didn't bother calling Mrs. McKenzie again. He knew all about her from his background check. She had, indeed, put a hefty second mortgage on her house for the center's security upgrades. He had to admire the lady. She put her entire life on the line for those kids.

He resolved to make sure the center was never mentioned in any news report. He would do whatever he could to make sure her reputation was not damaged.

Duncan put away his paperwork and cleaned off his desk. It was time to go home. Not that this case would ever leave his mind, but he needed a little time off, and tomorrow was it.

~~~

Sunday found him cleaning his house and doing laundry. His good friend, and fellow detective, Lou McGregor, who likes to harass him at work, only lived about three blocks away. Roger stood a full six foot tall, but Lou managed to raise him two more inches, which didn't happen often.

Roger called Lou hoping to have him over for lunch and discuss this case, but Lou had to work today. All detectives had to work one Sunday a month and it was Lou and his partner's turn. Maybe he could get his attention tomorrow at the station.

He decided to call Rocky and see how he was doing, but he wasn't going to dump any more trouble on his shoulders than his partner already had. He wanted an update and knew the captain would, too.

"Rocky, how's it going, bro?"

"Roger, you old dog. I was just thinking about you. For the life of me, I can't figure out how you are managing without me there!"

"Hey, I'm not, man. That's why I'm calling. When are you going to get off your lazy butt and come back to work? You can't skip out on your responsibilities forever!" Roger really liked his friend and partner. He was a good man.

"Jealousy is dripping all over you, partner, but I can certainly understand why it would be. I mean, after all, I get to lay around Dad's pool all day while you... just what *do* you do all day, anyway?"

After the joking stopped, Rocky told him

that his father, Sam, seemed to be doing better and he probably wouldn't be gone much longer.

He said he had spoken to Sam about maybe moving back to Wichita, and living with him. It was an option Rocky wanted his dad to keep open. Sam wouldn't be so lonely that way, plus the change of scenery could help him deal with the loss of his wife of forty-five years.

After chatting with his partner for a few more minutes and sharing a couple laughs over teaching his father how to do laundry, Roger hung up and returned to his own.

His friend, Lou, didn't do laundry. He had megabucks that Roger didn't have and hired a housekeeper to do his dirty work. He inherited it or something. Even his wealthy mother lived in this area. Darlene was a sweet lady. Roger was always teasing her to adopt him and get rid of Lou. She promised to think about it.

Darn it, so far it hasn't worked. Lord, do you think you could talk to her about that? She would listen to you! Roger smiled to himself.

But as for cleaning house, Roger didn't mind doing it at all. He loved his nice home in Woodlawn Village. It was a section of sprawling ranch style homes in East Wichita. Most had full basements and many had swimming pools, although his didn't. A swimming pool that is. Maybe someday, but not now.

A lot of them had circle drives too, including his. That was one of the selling points for him. His guests could park right by the front door. Not that he had many because he didn't, but maybe someday.

When he bought his house six years earlier, it was really more than he could afford. It took two years of scrimping and working extra as funeral escorts and security staff, to make the monthly payments. But with raises and promotions, he was now much better off and very pleased with his purchase. His four bedroom house was worth a lot more today than what he paid for it, but he never planned on selling. He loved his home.

The clean clothes went into the dryer, but he couldn't stop seeing Taylor's face. Sure she was a beautiful child, but it was something more. Something deeper.

Roger knew he was being haunted by her. She was inside him somehow. There was no other explanation. Why? He didn't know, but she was there. And as much loathing as he had for Adriana, he felt that much compassion for Angelina.

A quiet evening in front of the television was his reward for getting all of his work done. He was even able to get to bed early for a change.

However, Sunday night didn't go any better with his sleep. The nightmares wouldn't let up. He had to find her. He had to if he ever wanted to sleep at night again.

Chapter

7

At his desk on Monday, Roger was reading through his notes for what seemed like the tenth time, when he got a call from Linda, the woman who worked mornings at the Delano coffee shop.

"This is a surprise, Linda. What can I do for you?"

"Detective, I just thought you might want to know, Adriana has not been in for the past two days. The last time I saw her was Saturday morning. I know that sounds silly, but hear me out.

"That woman hasn't missed coming in every single day in the past two years. I mean she has *never* missed a day! But she wasn't in yesterday or today."

That got his attention. "Thank you for taking the time to let me know. I really appreciate it, Linda. I will look into it immediately." He said goodbye and hung up.

Well, now. Has our number one suspect flown the coop? Maybe she packed up and left in the middle of the night? Did she get tipped off that she was going to be arrested? I have to find this woman. She isn't going to get away with stealing Taylor.

On a hunch, Duncan got on the phone and called the law office. They reported that she didn't come in today. He was sure the receptionist sounded happy. When asked, she told him no one could remember the last time she missed work.

Looking at the background report for her home address, he ran for his car and headed to Eastborough, another small town swallowed by Wichita in years gone by. Though the small town relied on Wichita for their Fire Department, they still maintained their own police department. As a courtesy, he called them to meet him at her address. They agreed.

Once there, Duncan and two of Eastborough's police officers stood on her porch. When he rang the doorbell, there was no answer.

After ringing two more times to the same silence, Duncan asked the officers to search around the house while he searched the front area. Looking in windows that had drapes open was not easy as most of those in the front were higher up than usual. Then he heard the yell.

Eastborough officer, Bill Watkins was in the back yard and called everyone to come around.

Once together again, they looked into what appeared to be the family room's glass French doors.

Seeing past the room wasn't easy due to the very size of the room and the sunlight glare on the glass. Even with these restrictions, to the far left was what appeared to be the kitchen. You could just barely see something, or someone, lying on the floor.

Duncan told Watkins to contact his captain and get permission to enter, while he did the same.

Parry answered on the first ring.

"Captain, we are at the Mason home and there appears to be someone, or something, lying on the floor in the kitchen. I need permission to force entry."

"Can you see a body?"

"Well, something is lying on the floor. It

could be a body. The sun glare is keeping us from seeing any better." Duncan was getting irritated at the questions.

"No can do, Roger."

Parry told Duncan he couldn't force his way in without probable cause. Because something looked like it may be on the floor wasn't reason enough to break in.

"You can't be serious, captain?"

"I know. I know. For all we know, someone might have dropped a blanket on the floor. From what we have, I will try to get a warrant, but don't count on it."

Watkins also said he was denied the okay to break in. He said since we can't see for sure that it is a body, it was conjecture. Erroneous assumptions could get them sued by the homeowner if it turned out to be a dog lying there.

"Yeah, I know. I got the same crap. We're trying to get a warrant now."

Watkins said he couldn't stand there and wait. They would have to go back to their station.

After they left, Duncan slowly made his way around the house, checking every window, every door that he could. When he finally got back around to the French doors, the sun had moved a little and the glare was not as bad. Now he could see there was definitely someone lying on the floor. And it was not a dog.

Grabbing a large rock from the patio planter box, Duncan smashed in one of the glass doors so he could reach the lock and enter.

Thirty seconds later he was inside.

In the kitchen, face down on the floor, was the body of Adriana Mason. A large pool of blood was on the floor where she lay. It appeared she was stabbed to death from behind.

A bloody knife lay beside her. He obviously had the murder weapon. A single sunflower lay across her back, which seemed odd to Roger. Looking around the kitchen, he could find no other sunflowers.

Why would someone drop a flower on her back? Was that an accident? Or were they making a statement?

The body was cold to the touch, so she had been dead for a while.

He called Parry and explained the change in plans. He knew he would get chewed out for not waiting, but he wasn't going to worry about that now.

Parry ordered squads, CSI and the coroner to the property. While Duncan waited, he searched throughout the house to make sure there wasn't anyone else present.

When he confirmed he was alone, Roger turned his attention back to the kitchen where

Adriana was lying. Beautiful even in death. But without her stilettos, she looked so small, like her sister.

The sirens could be heard several blocks away. When they pulled up into the drive, Duncan opened the door for them. He explained what he saw, and what he found.

The police officers began searching the kitchen, they found baby food stocked up in one cabinet and the refrigerator was full of food that would appeal to any child. What was going on? This was a woman who hated children.

The EMTs waited while the coroner declared the woman dead. The CSI team starting taking pictures of the entire area. It was apparent she was killed in the kitchen because no blood or even drops were found anywhere else in the house. The knife was bagged as evidence.

Adriana must have known her killer because she turned away from the person. All of her stab wounds were in the back. It was also easy to see it was not premeditated. The killer grabbed one of the knives from the kitchen counter, making it appear a spontaneous act.

CSI was able to determine the killer was taller than Adriana because the wounds came from 'up to down' in strokes.

The yellow sunflower caused speculation by all. Was she in the kitchen looking for a vase, or did the killer leave it? No way to know at this time, but it too was carefully bagged.

~~~

One of the things Roger Duncan hated the most was informing the next of kin of a death, let alone when it was a murder. Even if the two were not close, telling her sister about Adriana won't be easy, especially with Taylor missing.

He drove to Angelina's apartment in the

early afternoon, knocked and waited. She opened the door and seemed glad to see him.

"Detective Duncan! Did you find Taylor?" Her voice was still like a whisper, but in her enthusiasm, it was almost a yell.

"Please call me Roger, Angelina. No, I haven't located Taylor, yet, however, I will. I promise you that." Duncan knew he shouldn't promise anything, but in his heart he knew this case would be solved if it took his last breath to do it.

When he entered, they both sat down next to each other on the couch. Angelina looked better, healthier even, than she did last week. Her resemblance to her sister was now very obvious.

He held her hands, hoping to help her through what he had to say.

For the next hour, he talked to her about Taylor, his suspicions about Adriana, and of course, her murder. Angelina cried over it all. He put his arm around her to hold her when she was suffering the most.

Roger knew her health would likely take a hit with all the bad news. He was surprised at how sad that made him. She really was a beautiful, kind-hearted lady. It boggled his mind to think of how different the two sisters were.

When Angelina was able to control herself again, he had to get back to work. Reiterating his previous promise, he told her he would find her little girl. He leaned over and kissed her on the forehead, then he left.

Roger didn't care if his kiss was inappropriate. She needed to know someone cared about her, especially now. He also knew she appreciated it.

Chapter

8

Adriana's death threw Roger Duncan's case into overload. He knew she was involved in the kidnapping, but now he had to find the other party, the one who obviously wanted to keep her quiet. As he compiled his information, the presence of the sunflower continued to bother him. Why it was there was important, but who put it there was most important.

Parry chewed him out for not waiting on a

warrant but admitted he would have done the same thing if he had seen a body.

All of the dead woman's phone and bank records were subpoenaed and he couldn't wait to get his hands on them. She had to have spoken with her accomplice at some time. Or, maybe there were several, Duncan just didn't know anything anymore. There was also how she or the accomplices were paid. The money had to be somewhere. Lots of it.

The coroner released the body after he had obtained all of the information available. The only way to solve this crime now was to concentrate on the crime scene and her lifestyle.

Tuesday's paper said there would be a funeral held for Adriana in three days, on Thursday. Duncan knew it would be an extravagant funeral, most likely paid for by her partner Derrick Porter, or the law firm itself.

As he was leaving the station, the media caught up with him.

"Detective, does Mason's death have anything to do with her missing niece? Did the daycare cent...."

Roger jumped on that. "I want to make one thing very clear. There was no daycare center involved. Adriana stated she had taken the child to one, however, we found out that was not true."

"Detective, you are saying Adriana Mason lied about the missing child?"

"Detective, who would want to kill an attorney. Do you think it could be a client?"

"Detective Duncan. How does the sister feel...."

That question just about dropped him. *How does the sister feel? Let's see, her baby is missing and her sister has been murdered. How the hell do you THINK she feels, you idiot?*

Without answering, he pushed his way down

the steps. They knew he couldn't comment on an open case. Why did the media have to be involved with every case he worked?

He headed back to Angelina's. Roger wanted to let her know he would be there, if she needed him.

When he arrived, she was a wreck. She was holding a picture of Taylor and crying hysterically. What mother wouldn't. He sat beside Angelina and held her tight as she cried. It was bad enough her sister was dead, but to not know where her little girl was had to be devastating. Roger's heart broke, too.

When she was able to control the tears, he promised, again, to find Taylor. Roger wanted her to know there was nothing that would stop him from bringing her baby back to her.

After moments of silence, Angelina sat up straight. She put her hand on his cheek when he offered to take her to her sister's funeral if she felt up to going.

"That is very kind of you, Roger. I thank you and I accept. Not very many women can be seen with such a handsome man. I will be the envy of the event." He blushed at her compliment, pleased to see her small smile. Then she spoke in a small raspy voice

"Roger, I know she wasn't the best sister in the world, but she was the only one I had. I knew she felt different about everything than I do, but I didn't see anything wrong with her being different. Obviously, my main concern is what happened to Taylor. My heart can't take much more pain."

He was always amazed at how kind she could be to the woman who stole her child. Without thinking, he once again kissed her forehead before he left. He made arrangements to take Thursday off, so he could spend some time with Angelina, making sure she got through the day okay.

Duncan had promised to take her out to

dinner that evening. He was pretty sure she had not been out since her husband died. And he also knew it would probably be her last time. Besides, he wanted to.

He spent the afternoon scheduling each of the law firm employees to come in for an interview the next day, Wednesday, then went home.

~~~

The following morning, one after another, those who had worked for, or with, her came in. Porter gave each of them permission to leave work for their assigned appointments, but Duncan figured he didn't do it just to please the detective.

First in was the receptionist, Stephanie Weathers.

"She was very difficult to work with. You bowed and kissed her feet or you were unemployed. She looked down on all of us peons. Well, you saw that for yourself, didn't you. I loved how you stood up to her.

"No, I don't know of any work that has come in that involved children. Believe me, Adriana would not have taken that case."

~~~

Next was Adriana's personal secretary, Elizabeth Blackburn. Everyone called her Betty.

"I took her abuse like everyone else, but I'm in my fifties now, so I was just biding time until retirement. No one will miss Adriana, that's for sure, unless it is her latest screw. Men fantasized about her because they were only thinking between their legs. They wouldn't have had anything to do with her if they knew her at all.

"No, I didn't know she had a niece. It doesn't surprise me that I didn't know because that woman hated children.

~~~

After Betty, Derrick Porter's personal secretary came in.

"I would not have worked for her for all the money in China. Nothing is worth being verbally abused every day of your life. I just stayed out of her way and did my job for Derrick. He's wonderful to work for."

Duncan wondered just how wonderful he was to her. He finally had a break for lunch and took advantage of it. He went to his favorite Chinese place and grabbed some take out.

~~~

Back at his desk, he was finishing lunch and going over what each of the morning appointments had to say when the next one showed up, Legal Assistant, David Simon.

"Well, she was something to look at, but you know, her beauty taught me to love average looking women. Seriously. Someone that beautiful is so self-centered that it's a real turnoff. I want my woman to be real. You know, live in the real world where you are nice and considerate to others. A woman who knows the world does not revolve around her. I'll take that woman over the Adrianas any day."

~~~

Waiting for him when David left was the other Legal Assistant, Chelsea Baker.

"When she was around, I just locked myself in the law library. My assignments were texted to me anyway, so I could avoid having to be around her, which is exactly the way I wanted it. Sorry, but whoever killed her, did us all a favor. She was the meanest witch in town."

Roger came back with, "Did she ever have

you research anything to do with children?"

"You're kidding, right? Adriana hated kids and let everyone know it."

~~~

The Office Manager, Mrs. Jessica Kendall, was next.

"I kept my job by doing it well and keeping my mouth shut and that is what I am going to do now. I don't know anything about her murder and you can't say I did."

~~~

Now it was time to visit with the last one on his list, the night janitor, J. D. Colter. When he walked into the interview room, Duncan stopped in his tracks. There sat someone he knew, the night janitor for the day care center, Lester Calvin.

"This says your name is J. D. Colter. What is this?" Duncan jumped on this guy. "What kind of scam are you pulling here?"

"Hey, I knew if I told you I was also the night janitor for Mason's law firm, you would jump to conclusions!"

"Now, let's see, a child supposedly goes missing from a place you work and it is known that the person who owns the second place you work is responsible and you think I am jumping to conclusions?" He was leaning over Lester's face, getting angrier by the minute.

"Okay, okay. I see your point, but I didn't have nuthin to do with it. I swear, man. I only met the woman once. She was working late and I was surprised to see a light on in her office. When I finished everything else, I knocked. She said 'enter' so I opened the door and asked her if she would be much longer so I could clean up, ya know, and empty the trash an' all.

"She seemed in a mellow enough mood and asked me to sit and talk with her a moment. What am I gonna tell her, no? So I sat down. She asked me about my job, did I like it, and so on. I told her I also worked for the Kansas Kidz Center at night, cleaning up. She seemed really interested when I said that, but also told me she wasn't too keen on kids and we laughed about that.

"Then she said something that really surprised me. She asked why I didn't use a different name for each job. I didn't really understand what she meant. Why would I need another name?

"Well, she said it was perfectly legal to use as many names as you wanted to, just as long as it wasn't for fraud reasons, ya know? I wasn't even sure what that meant, but I just nodded and agreed with whatever she said. After all, she was the lawyer, ya know?

"She said she could use a guy like me every now and then. If I was interested in making more money, then I should consider the second name thing. Well, I ain't stupid, so I said, yeah, I would like to make more money. She said good and said she would set it all up, then she left. I cleaned up her office and left, too.

"After that, I started getting paid as J. D. Colter. I had a bank account and everything." Lester just shrugged like it was acceptable.

"What did she have you doing for her?" Angry, but contained, Roger watched every twitch and blink from this guy.

"Nothing. I mean that was only two weeks ago and she never had any extra work for me, at least not yet. And now she's dead, so I don't figure there will ever be any.

"That was it, I never saw her in person again."

Duncan saw the truth in some of that and

knew he didn't have anything to keep this guy on. Was Adriana setting up this smuck to deliver stolen kids? Hard to tell, but he wasn't letting him off the hook just yet.

"Don't leave town, Lester. I mean it. You better be available if I have any more questions. I am not through with you yet. Stop using that fake name, and close that phony bank account. You inform the law firm to pay you as before."

"Sure. I understand and I don't plan on going nowhere."

Lester Calvin left as Duncan watched him go out the door.

The only one who couldn't make it in was a teenage boy, Terry Gates, who worked part-time as a mail clerk. Duncan got him on the phone between classes. Seems the boy was rather enamored by her looks and would dream about her. Yeah, Duncan had a pretty good idea what kind of dreams a teenager would have about a beautiful woman.

Looking back over them all, He was amused to find most of them were eager to let him know what they thought of their boss. Seems not a one that knew her, liked her very much, whereas Porter was a perfectly nice guy.

He wanted to find out more about her partner. Somehow he doubted Derrick Porter was all that nice.

They put together a picture of Adriana being self-serving, egotistical, demeaning and demanding. Well, that was pretty much how he found her, too. Oh yeah, and a good liar to boot.

But none of the employees had a motive for kidnapping her niece–especially since no one even knew she had one. Outside of work, there were no ties of any kind. Duncan was getting tired of dead ends.

Lord, everyone seems to be glad she's gone, but no one had reason to kill her....

Reading reports take time and Duncan was

not known for his patience. He had a bad habit of pacing the floor at the station when thinking or reading through his cases. Eventually some other detective shouted at him to sit down because he was driving them crazy.

Pacing was what he was doing now. This time it was his friend, Lou, who threw an eraser at him.

He sat back down, still enthralled by his case.

Chapter

9

The next day, he picked Angelina up to attend her sister's funeral. He was shocked when she opened the door. She looked stunning. She was in a pretty dress, makeup applied perfectly and a long, dark wig made her a real head turner. Her normally red, swollen eyes were expertly disguised with makeup.

Yes, she was definitely Adriana's twin. Where he looked at the dead woman's beauty with disgust, her sister's made his heart pound. Even in a wheelchair, she looked great.

Roger Duncan just stared at her until she smiled and invited him in. He was pretty sure his cheeks were red hot.

He wanted to take Angelina to the funeral for two reasons. To make sure she was able to go to her sister's funeral was certainly the main reason. She now spent half her time in a wheel chair because she was too weak to walk. He didn't care one bit. Pushing the chair was no problem for him.

The second was to see everyone who came to see Adriana off. It doesn't always happen, but many times the killer is at the service.

Why do they show up at the funeral? I have no clue. Maybe they are just making sure the vic is dead.

Before leaving, she put on a veiled hat and large sunglasses.

"I don't want people seeing me since I look like Adriana. This is her day, not mine."

When they arrived the stares at Angelina were common place. A woman in a wheel chair, wearing a veil of mourning, just didn't fit the deceased. After all, Adriana had no known family, so who was this lady quietly sobbing?

Duncan watched the crowd and several men stood out. One was a well-dressed young man who didn't look like he could be over thirty. Duncan recognized him from his picture in the paper. It was her business partner, Derrick Porter.

He seemed to be in his own little world, not noticing anything around him. Was he that attached to Adriana that he can't bear the loss? Or was it something else. He would check on that possibility later.

Another was Wichita's own Mayor, Marcus Warden, and a State Senator, Jeffrey Henderson. How did they know her well enough to come to her funeral? No doubt about it, Roger was going to have to do more digging. Why would they be at the funeral of such a self-serving narcissist? It was something he had to find out, but not today.

Per Angelina's request, they stayed to the back of the crowd. She didn't want her tears to bring any attention to herself.

Right after the services, Roger took Angelina home so she could take a nap and rest. He told her he would be back for her at seven for dinner.

He spent the afternoon at home, making notes as to those he saw at the funeral. The mayor, the senator, all of them. He knew he would have to talk with each of them, in time.

When Roger returned to Angelina's that evening, she was, once again, a beautiful sight to see. This time, she was not in a wheel chair. She said she wanted to make it on her own, one last time. The woman was positively radiant, and no longer looked like a mourner.

They went to the Steak and Ale Restaurant where they ate and talked for almost three hours. They avoided subjects that might be painful. Tonight was for her to enjoy, not hurt, but it was also one of the most enjoyable evenings Roger could ever remember.

When he took her home, he knew she had his heart, and there was nothing he could do about it. He was head over heels in love with her, and she was going to die.

He kissed her on the cheek and said goodbye. Though her eyes were sad, she gave him a little smile.

When he got his broken heart home, he cried until the tears wouldn't come anymore, then fell into a fitful sleep.

~~~

Friday morning found the detective deep in thought back at his desk. He had to keep his mind off of Angelina if he was going to solve this complicated case.

Did Adriana know about Derrick's jury tampering? Did she have proof? Did she blackmail him over it so he had to kill her? Worse yet, was he the one who took Taylor from her behind the coffee shop? That man and I need a face to face.

One ex-employee, Mike Faller, filed sexual harassment charges against her, saying she demanded to have sex with him, then fired him. Wow. I think I would be pissed, too. Gotta check him out.

The receptionist said she had lunch with the Mayor, Marcus Warden, almost every week. He was in his forties and she was a knockout in her early thirties...Was there an affair going there? Maybe even blackmail? An appointment with him was in order.

Over and over, every angle ran through his brain until his head started to pound. He took some aspirins and left for lunch. Maybe this afternoon would be easier.

When Duncan returned, the sunshine and fresh air had helped to clear his mind, plus his pounding headache was gone. The first thing he did was make an appointment with Derrick Porter for an hour later.

There were two new reports on his desk. One was the background on all the people involved in any part of her life, that they were aware of, and the other was the list of phone calls made on Adriana's business, home and cell phones. He didn't want to leave anything, or anyone, out.

There wasn't time to go over them now, but he would when he got back this afternoon. He dropped them into one of his desk drawers and went to the captain's office to let him know he would be leaving.

He decided to drive, even though it was only a few blocks because this wouldn't be his only appointment for the day.

When Duncan arrived, a happy looking Stephanie was still sitting at the reception desk. She literally bubbled.

"Good afternoon, Detective Duncan. So nice to see you again. How may I help you today?"

He told her of his appointment with Porter and this time she called his office and told him Duncan was there.

Porter showed up within seconds to escort him into a very lavish office.

"Sit down, detective. I am always glad to help out the WPD when I can. I have to assume you are here about Adriana?"

"Yes. When did you see her last?"

"I last saw Adriana on Monday. I had to leave on a business trip to Oklahoma, for a client that day, so I wasn't here two days later when you came in to see her."

Porter was anticipating Duncan's next question and was trying to answer first.

"I was in Oklahoma City for a week. As always with clients, I charged everything on my corporate card so the client could be charged for all expenses, therefore I can prove my whereabouts."

Duncan looked at him and said, "That doesn't mean you couldn't have had someone else kill Adriana for you. Everyone knows your client list falls in the 'Who's Who of Low Life's' around here." It was a long shot, but certainly a possibility.

Porter's brows went up and he laughed, "I had no reason to kill her. She and I were making a fortune off our clients. I can't do all of this alone! Now I will have to hire someone to help out. To think I would want her gone is ludicrous."

"Rumor has it you were her boyfriend."

"Well, the rumors are right, at least for about 4 months. After that we just settled in as friends and colleagues. Adriana is not the easiest person to get along with. And it didn't take long to realize money was her first, and only love." Porter was enjoying himself.

"Did you break it off?"

"No, actually, she did. That was about eighteen months ago. But I was very happy to accommodate her. Adriana did not want to be tied down, for any reason. And I didn't want to be tied down to her! So we parted as good friends and colleagues."

"I heard an ex-employee filed sexual harassment charges against her and the firm." Duncan definitely wanted to hear more about this.

"Aw, yes. Mike. Well, I don't know much about it. He said she demanded sex from him and then fired him. She said she never had sex with him, that she did fire him for lousy work, and that he was just trying to get a big financial reward.

"Detective, I don't know much more than that. Was she the type to do that to him. Yes. But is he the type to make it all up for a big payday? I don't know, maybe yes, again." Porter was taking all of this lightly.

He went on, "I have to admit, Adriana and I did have one discussion about Mike, and it was a bit racy. My secretary told me about something that she had heard about Mike. Seems he took out a gal from the law firm two floors down and they got it on. Well, the fast flying rumor was that he was 'incredibly endowed,' especially for his short stature.

"I passed that on to my partner when we were laughing about some of the other antics our employees pull. Did that make her want to try it? I don't know, detective. I don't even try to figure out women anymore, let alone Adriana."

Duncan jumped in, "Since the suit wasn't

settled yet, he didn't have any reason to kill her, so we are back to you. Maybe she was blackmailing you." He wasn't going to let up.

"Bla...whatever for, Detective?"

"Maybe you helped her kidnap children."

"Are you serious, detective? I have no idea what you are talking about. No one is kidnapping children that I know of!" He laughed the idea away.

"Then you are saying you are not aware of her activities in stealing children? How could you *not* know?"

Finally seeing Duncan was serious, Porter stopped smiling and said, "Detective, I do *not* have any idea what Adriana did with her off time and I didn't follow her around eavesdropping on her phone calls, and I have *no* idea about any children missing. This is certainly the first I have heard about any of that."

116

"That doesn't mean she still wasn't blackmailing you. Maybe she knew something about the charges brought against you last year. Maybe she threatened to tell on you."

At the mention of last year's charges made against him, he turned cold and said, "Detective, be careful where you tread. I was not charged with anything."

"Oh, I know you weren't. I was just speculating why you might want Adriana dead."

"Well, I didn't want her dead. Now if you will excuse me, I have to get back to work." He leaned over his desk to the intercom: "Stephanie, will you come and escort the detective out?"

Duncan left not learning much more than he knew when he walked in. Except maybe that bit about Faller.

Nice going, Duncan.

Now, it was time to see what Mike Faller

had to say. He was now working for a law firm located on Webb Road, the far east side of the city. Duncan had agreed to meet with him at a nearby restaurant.

Chapter

10

Sitting across from Mike Faller in the restaurant was certainly an eye opening experience. He was a guy only a few inches taller than Adriana, maybe five-five. Yes, he was attractive, but he couldn't weigh more than one-hundred-forty pounds. He just didn't seem to be the type Adriana would pick for a sexual contact.

Then add her five-inch stilettos and she would be taller than Mike. But then, who wears shoes when having sex, anyway?

But, at this point, he wouldn't put anything past her, and there's the rumor Porter told her about.

"It is all in the law suit I filed. Exactly as it happened," Mike said. He sounded annoyed.

"We had worked after hours one day and we were alone in the office. She called me in from her intercom, and I was worried. Worried because when she calls in an employee, it is usually to blame them for some trivial problem she thinks is a mountain, or to chew them out for some stupid reason. *Pleasing* Adriana Mason did *not* appear on any of our resumes, I can assure you of that.

"Anyway, I opened the door to her office and she was naked from the waist up! I mean really! Her breasts were bare and she was in the process of removing everything from the waist down. I stood and stared for a second until she said in this sexy voice, 'Mike come here. I need you.'

"Well, I am not stupid. This woman was a goddess to look at. At least until she opens her mouth. Okay, so I go up to her and she starts undressing me and touching me between the legs. Believe me, it didn't take long to become personally involved, if you get my drift.

"We really went at it. I'm telling you, she threw me down on the couch and jumped on top of me. When we finished there, she laid on the floor with her legs spread and I jumped on top of her! I can tell you, I wasn't thinking about tomorrow or even who she was.

"Yeah, I know. I was thinking below the belt. But believe me, she was moaning and groaning, too! She couldn't get enough of me and wouldn't stop. After about two hours of trying every surface of her office, she finally let me go. I was actually grateful. I didn't know how much longer I could keep up the pace, if you know what I mean.

"She started getting dressed and so I took the hint and did the same. After I was dressed, I left her office and went back to my desk.

When she came out of her office about fifteen minutes later, she was all put together again and you would never know what just happened. I smiled at her with all my great memories. But that smile didn't last long.

"She came up to my desk and said, 'You're fired. Clear everything out of your desk right now.' Man, I thought she was kidding. She walked away and left. I know she has a weird sense of humor, so I just thought that was a stupid thing to say.

"Next thing I know, there is a security guard at my desk. He tells me she instructed him to clear out my things, take my security card and escort me to the door! For real! And that's what he did.

"I have to tell you, detective, I was stunned. I tried to call her but she wouldn't take my calls.

I received my last paycheck in the mail.

"After about a month of messages being ignored, I filed the lawsuit. I knew I didn't have much of a chance to win. I mean, it is a 'he said, she said' anyway. Plus, I know I am not the person everyone would expect to see her with. I know that. Maybe that is why she picked me. I don't know.

"So there you have it, detective. Now that she is gone, I have no case. Really. How can I possibly prove something like that. Pissed, yes. But killing her would have taken away my only chance of making her pay for what she did to me." Mike Faller looked sad, almost despondent.

"Mike, can you think of anyone who might want to do her harm? Anyone at all?" Duncan knew it was worth a shot.

"I have asked myself that same question. I don't have any idea about her life outside the office, and certainly nothing recently since I don't work there. But I heard a really bad

123

argument between her and Porter about a week before I was fired. It wasn't the first time, so I didn't think much about it. They certainly had their differences."

"Did you hear what the argument was about?"

"Naw. Those offices are almost sound proof. That is why you knew something bad was going on if voices were loud enough to be heard outside the doors."

Detective Duncan thanked Mike for talking with him. He picked up the check and went to the front to pay.

Faller was right. His case was pretty much over since her death. And that takes the focus off of him as the killer. For now, anyway. No one could be written off permanently. But Duncan would bet his badge Faller didn't do it.

He walked out of that restaurant more disgusted with Adriana than before, if that was even possible.

~~~

Late afternoon, Duncan caught his friend Lou alone at his desk. Seems his partner, Donna Decker, was off interviewing someone on their current case. Lou was going over the files.

Sitting down at Donna's desk, which faced Lou's, he asked his friend if he had a moment.

"You bet, Rog. What's up?" Lou was a handsome light-skinned African American, who was obsessed with dressing to the nines. Roger didn't think he could remember ever seeing Lou in anything except two thousand dollar suits, except when he was invited over to his house or his mother's for a bar-b-q. His wardrobe would be casual, but still expensive. Roger didn't think the man even owned a pair of jeans.

Lou's partner was a stunning woman who made heads turn no matter where she was. Most of the guys on the squad envied him, but Roger didn't because Lou was such a good friend.

"A three-year-old girl is missing. Her aunt was the one who caused it to happen, but someone killed the aunt. I'm at a loss where to go from here. What do you think, my friend."

Lou looked back at him. Roger knew what he was thinking. Nothing is worse than a case where the victim is a child. They had all been there and it was never pretty.

Lou stared silently at him for several minutes. Duncan just waited while it all sifted through his friend's brain.

"I know it sounds corny, Rog, but follow the money," Lou finally stated.

"I hear that Lou, but there isn't any. The mother is poor and in bad health. And, no one has asked for ransom."

"No, the other end. Whoever took her would

have to benefit somehow or it would not be worth their time. If it isn't financial, it's *personal*. Don't overlook that angle either. What about the child's father? An ugly custody problem, maybe?"

Duncan got up and smiled. "Thanks, my friend. There are no known relatives and the father is deceased. I have already subpoenaed everyone's bank and phone records but they haven't come in yet. I just needed another point of view to let me know if I was in the right direction."

Lou smiled, "Oh, you definitely are, which doesn't surprise me a bit. Say, what's up with Rocky. When is he coming back?"

He told Lou everything he knew about Rocky's circumstances but didn't have a date when he would return.

"Lou, how is that wonderful mother of yours doing?" Duncan was fond of Darlene. Everyone knew it. "Has she decided to adopt me yet?"

"Oh, she is doing great. And, you may have a chance at that adoption yet! She says I have been a lousy son since I haven't given her any grandchildren to play with. I know she gets lonely in that house all by herself."

Lou continued, "Call me old fashion, but I would rather get married before I have children!" Both laughed at the usual complaint of a mother.

"Well, there went my adoption. I don't have any kids, either!" They both laughed and Duncan returned to his desk. Time to pull all of the reports from his drawer.

First, he skimmed over the backgrounds of all the employees from the day care and the law firm. Nothing out of the ordinary and nothing worse than an old DUI.

Then he pulled out the phone records. Those he took over to Stanley, the computer guru who helped the detectives whenever he could.

"Stanley, I need all of these phone numbers

cross checked. I want to know any numbers that match from the other lists and eliminate any that belong to this list of clients. How long to do you think it will take."

"Give me until the morning. I'll see what I can do." Stanley smiled.

"As always, you da man, Stan." Duncan was sure those numbers would help.

Chapter

11

Roger heard his phone ringing as he returned to his desk. He grabbed it before the caller hung up.

"Duncan."

"Is this Detective Duncan? The one investigating the death of Adriana Mason?"

He jumped on it. "Yes, Ma'am, I am. How

can I help you?"

"Well," the woman said, " My name is Carol Parker. I am... or was, her housekeeper and I need to have access to the house again to get my personal belongings out. I have a key, but I noticed the yellow tape around the doors and I certainly didn't want to break the law. Can you help me?"

"You bet! I will meet you there in twenty minutes! Is that okay?"

"Yes, I will wait here."

Duncan grabbed Adriana's keys from her file, gave the captain a ten-second update and ran for the door. He was so excited to find someone who could tell him what went on in that house.

Why didn't he think of a housekeeper before? Adriana wasn't the kind to risk breaking a fingernail!

When he pulled up to Mason's house in

Eastborough, there was a stocky woman standing at the front door. She looked to be mid-forties.

He parked and ran for the door, then introduced himself.

"Hello, detective. I'm Carol Parker, Adriana's housekeeper. I had the day off when she died, so I didn't come back until the next day. No one was here but the 'do not enter' tape was. So I waited for days before coming back, but the tape is still here."

"Hello, Ms. Parker. Very nice to meet you! Come on, I will let you in." He ripped off the tape and put the key into the door. They both walked in. The alarm had not been set because no one knew the code.

When he asked her about the alarm, she gave him the code which he wrote down. He would be sure to set it when he left so no one would try to loot the place now that it was vacant.

"What personal property do you have here, Ms. Parker?"

"I always kept some extra clothes here and some makeup. Adriana didn't like for me to look worn out, so if I got dirty or needed a touch-up, I could do it. It is in the maid's quarters in the garage. It's fully furnished, of course, so none of that is mine."

"Before we go there, what can you tell me about what she did with her time at home?"

Carol sighed and said, "Well, it was interesting, I can tell you that. I have been in this business most of my life and never have I had an employer like Ms. Mason.

"About once a month, she would bring home a child and have me take care of it. Some would be malnourished and some would be bruised where they had been beaten. I don't know where she found these kids, but it sure was a good thing she did. Some wouldn't have made it much longer."

"Did she have any male callers here?"

"No. Oh, I know she 'liked' men, if you get my drift, but this house was just not the place to bring them to, not with all the kids coming and going. I guess she met them elsewhere. She would usually tell me if she wasn't coming home that night."

"What would you do with the children if she didn't come home?"

"Oh, if there was a child here, I couldn't go home, even if she *was* here. I was the only one who took care of them.

"You see, detective, I am a widow and I don't have anyone at home who needs me. I have a grown son, but he is off doing his thing and I am alone. She would pay me extra for all the times I had to stay all night, and I didn't mind. It was fun, actually, watching these little creatures, getting some life back in them after such a rough start. And they would sleep with me. And truth be known, I needed the money from this job."

He showed her the picture of Taylor and asked her if this was one of the children.

"Goodness, no. This child looks as healthy as can be. Pretty thing, too."

Duncan walked her out back and opened the garage with one of the keys on Mason's key chain. Once inside the maid's quarters, he was surprised at how large the whole apartment was.

There was a living room, almost luxurious, with a flat screen TV. A kitchenette made it possible to have some food and drinks. The bedroom was outfitted with a high-end full sized bed and a crib. The bathroom had all the needed amenities, even a walk-in shower.

It was well furnished and decorated. He almost chuckled at the thought. Adriana even had to have her housekeeper living better than any others.

He helped Carol Parker remove her things and put them in her car. He took her phone number and address, just in case he had more questions. Carol gave Roger the house keys and he dropped them in his pocket. He thanked her for her help before she drove off.

After she left, he wondered through the house trying to think like the owner. What did Adriana think of this or that? Then he set the alarm, locked up and left. The day was quickly flying by and he had another appointment to keep this afternoon.

~~~

At exactly three o'clock on Wednesday afternoon, he was outside the door to Mayor Marcus Warden's office.

Roger Duncan was not going to accuse the Mayor of being crooked or having an affair without a whole lot more evidence, so he had to watch what he said and how he said it. Taking a deep breath, he went through the door.

He was shown into the mayor's office

immediately. The Mayor was sitting behind his desk, piled with the work of the day.

"Detective Duncan, is it? Nice to meet you. What can I do for you?" Warden had some Hispanic heritage as he looked the part, but his name didn't fit. He was well educated and his English was impeccable, indicative of mix heritage. That pretty much fit everyone these days.

He had been mayor of Wichita for over ten years and had done what seemed like an excellent job. He was highly regarded by the people, so Duncan hoped upon hope that he didn't find out anything that would rip the city apart.

"Mr. Mayor, thank you for seeing me on such short notice. I want to talk to you about your acquaintance with Adriana Mason."

"Oh yes. Horrible thing that was, detective. Any idea who could have done such a terrible thing?"

"Not yet, Mr. Mayor, but we are definitely working on it. Can you tell me how you happen to know her?" Duncan was carefully watching Warden's face for any sign of nervousness. He found none.

"Of course. She had helped a couple of friends of mine with their personal problems, so I was grateful for her friendship."

"Do you mind telling me what those personal problems were?" Duncan felt like he was getting somewhere.

"Uh, well, since my friends used her as their attorney, I don't feel right about divulging their reasons for using her services. I hope you understand, detective."

He did. It was a long shot anyway. "So you had lunch with her on a fairly regular basis, then?"

"I tried to. I mean, she would have her secretary call mine about once a week for lunch and I would fit her in when I could. It was nice, actually to get away from people who are part of my workday and have lunch with someone that just wanted to talk about the weather and such. And was beautiful to boot!" The mayor chuckled.

"But, like I said, it was only about once a week or so, because a mayor's work follows him most of the time, if you get my drift. Sometimes lunch has to be included in the work schedule."

Duncan understood completely. Now it was time to get a little more personal and he needed to do it very carefully.

"Did you know anything about her personal life, Mr. Mayor?"

"No, I don't think so. I am trying to remember if she ever said anything. You know, I don't even know if she was married or not. She didn't talk about herself in personal ways, only professional. You know, how heavy her client load was, how well her partner was doing, that sort of thing." Marcus Warden didn't seem to have any problems talking about his relationship with the dead woman.

"Can you think of anyone who would want to hurt her? Did she ever tell you about someone who threatened her? Anything along those lines?" Duncan wasn't expecting much here, but you never know.

"Well, I… Detective Duncan, I ask that you keep this in complete confidence. Agreed?"

"I will if I can, sir. You have my word." Now Duncan was sitting upright and all ears.

"Well, the only person that I ever heard her say anything negative about was her partner."

"Porter? Derrick Porter?"

"Yes, that's him. Anyway, you are probably aware of his problems with the law last year. Well, it seems, Adriana was mortified at what he had done and wanted him out of the firm, but he refused to leave and threatened to ruin her if she tried to get him out. She told me she was a bit afraid of him."

"Mr. Mayor, do you know anything about the friendship or relationship between Adriana and State Senator Jeffrey Henderson? I noticed he was at the funeral services, too."

"No, actually. I know he speaks highly of her legal abilities and all, but I don't know if he is a client of hers or not. It certainly wouldn't be unusual for a politician to keep an attorney on retainer." Both the mayor and Roger laughed.

The mayor went on, "Truthfully, that is all I know, Detective Duncan. And I apologize but I have a meeting in ten minutes. Do find her killer, detective. This has to be solved."

"Yes, sir. I feel the same way. I appreciate your time, and I will show myself out."

Duncan decided not to go straight back to the station. He drove around for a while throwing all of the information up in the air and trying to see where it fell.

He was again back at Porter. Did her partner get rid of her because she threatened to kick him out of the firm? She could have legally done that on the charge of 'misconduct' under the law. Is that what Mike heard them arguing about?

Derrick Porter just went back to the top of his suspect list for killing Adriana.

But what about Taylor? Could the two cases actually be separate after all? A coincidence of time and space? Adriana sold Taylor for money and Porter killed her for the law firm?

Roger didn't drink much, but he knew it was a good thing he didn't have a bottle of bourbon with him because he felt like he could have put it to good use.

Chapter

12

After consulting with the captain, Parry ordered surveillance on Porter. If Adriana was afraid of him, there was probably a good reason. There was a trace put on his home and cell phones as well as a monitor on his bank accounts.

There was one more issue to address this afternoon, and that was speaking with State Senator Jeffery Henderson. He was in his mid-thirties and serving his first term for the State of Kansas.

Since he lived and worked in the state capital of Topeka, Duncan knew his best bet was by Skype. He called the senator's office and informed them to prepare for his call. He then went into the media room and turned on the computer. After logging into Skype, he contacted the senator.

To his surprise, he made contact on the first try and immediately put through. Senator Henderson's face came up on the monitor.

"What can I do for you, detective?" That's a politician for you. Straight to the point. But at least he was smiling.

"First, I want to thank you for taking the time to speak with me. I know you must be very busy…"

'No problem, detective, and call me Jeff. So what's up?"

"And Roger, please Jeff. I noticed you were at the funeral of a Wichita attorney, Adriana Mason. I was wondering if you could explain how you two know each other." Duncan was putting it as mildly as he could. No need to offend the guy, right?

"No problem, Roger. Adriana and I were lovers. At least for about six months or so. She was just too ambitious for me, I guess. Gorgeous, but she had a dark side. She didn't seem to care how she made money, as long as she did.

"I have to tell you, it scared me sometimes. If I mentioned a problem at the office, she would offer ways to 'fix' it and most of the time, those 'ways' were illegal. At first, I thought she was just joking around, but after a while, it became obvious that is how she would handle things. I just didn't want her in my life anymore.

"Anyway, after about six months or so, I broke it off. She didn't like it one bit. I am sure she thought dating a State Senator would somehow benefit her law firm, but I was not interested in her lack of morals.

"I have since met a lovely woman whose only ambition is my career and that is just what a politician needs, isn't it? We both fell hard and have been engaged for two months.

"However, just because I didn't want to be personally involved with her, didn't mean I didn't know her. I mean, it is hard not to appreciate a woman who looks like that, right, Roger? And she was a legal whiz kid.

"When I heard about her death, of course I was going to pay my respects."

Duncan never expected a straightforward answer coming from, well, a politician. He got straight to the point and told him the truth. *Wow. Maybe he will get my vote at the next election.*

"Jeff, do you know of anyone who may want to hurt her?"

"Not a one. But that doesn't mean much, Roger, because I didn't know much about her Wichita life when we were together, and certainly not anything since we broke up."

"I thank you for your time, and your honesty, Jeff. You have been very helpful. Have a good day." Duncan closed the connection and watched the computer monitor go dark. He sat quietly for a long time.

The woman had no morals and certainly lacked in class. All the things her twin sister had. Mind boggling. He would never think about twins the same again.

Wrapping up the day, Roger updated the captain before heading home. He grabbed some takeout chicken and pulled into his garage. That's when he knew there was a problem.

When Duncan stopped his car in his garage, he could see the door into his house was open. It should not be open. It was locked and the alarm system was on when he left this morning.

His training kicked in and he backed his car out of the garage, called for backup and waited. All of that 'barging in alone with their gun drawn to take on the bad guy' was Hollywood malarkey. Most cops were not that stupid. And that is how they stayed alive.

Two squad cars arrived at the same time. With guns drawn, four police officers entered the house and looked into every room and closet. The house had been ransacked, but no one was there.

What could anyone be looking for? Or were they just trying to scare me? How dare someone invade my personal space! Scare me, they didn't, but piss me off, they certainly did!

The garage door had not been broken into, so it looked like someone had a key. They must have come in through the garage walk-out door. How could that be? He never gave anyone a key to his house. The alarm system had been turned off, but no one else knew that code. However, it appears that someone now has both.

Were vengeful gang members trying to get to him? Captain Parry wouldn't take no for an answer again and assigned a car to watch his house for a few days.

The worst thing was the spray paint on his living room wall. "You'll be sorry" was scrawled along a ten-foot area. What he would be sorry for was unknown. When you are a cop, it could be anything. But putting two child killers in prison seemed to be a good start.

Sedgwick County CSI arrived and spent two hours dusting everything they could find for prints. No one thought they would find any, but they had to try. Unfortunately, they were right.

After everyone left, Roger spent the next several hours trying to put everything he owned back into its proper place. What a mess. Even silverware was thrown from the drawers. Someone really wanted to ruin his day.

Through it all, he only found one thing missing. About five thousand in cash he kept in a ceramic pot in his dining room china cabinet. Since the whole place was trashed, it appeared they may have been looking for that one thing. But no one knew he had money in his home, or was it just assumed a cop would keep some cash around? That made sense, unfortunately.

After altering his alarm code and making sure it was set, he was in bed by midnight. No playing chess tonight. It didn't take him long to fall asleep. Exhaustion will do to that to you.

~~~

The following morning, Roger called in and got permission to come in late while getting all of his locks changed. Having changed the alarm code, changing the locks would make him feel secure again.

While the locksmith was working around his house on all the doors to the outside, he painted over the words on the wall in the living room. He felt violated. After all, this was his home. The faster he could get things back to normal, the better.

When he arrived at work two hours later than normal, he briefed the captain on the money he found missing. He also let him know his home seemed to be secure again. Then he sat down at his desk to do the paperwork on his own breaking and entering. A B&E could not get more personal than this.

Just when he thought he was through with paperwork, Stanley dropped a folder on his desk and left. It took a moment or two for Duncan to remember what it was about. The phone logs!

For the next two hours he went over and over each one. Since all clients phone numbers were omitted, he only had about thirty to deal with. It was the calls made on her personal number that he was most interested in.

One, with multiple calls, was her hair

dresser. Another, her manicurist. Figures. We have to look perfect at all times, don't we? Similar calls to a seamstress. He called just to convince himself it wasn't a bogus number. The lady on the other end told him she altered all of Adriana's clothes to match her tiny waist. Seems she spent more with the seamstress than she did on her hair.

Checking on others, he discovered she had a thing for Chinese food and would order take out several times a week. Guess she took it home.

A lot of calls went to a name what was a bit familiar. When he did a reverse check, he discovered it was a local private investigator, Lana Carter.

It wasn't unusual for an attorney to have a private detective on speed dial, but Duncan felt he ought to check it out anyway. One thing that made these calls suspicious was the fact they only showed up on her private number, never the business phone. He dialed the number and left a message for Lana to call him back.

There was another call he needed to make. He had a snitch that helped him with the gang case and he may know who is after him.

"Roberto, how's it going? Say, I am having some problems with damages at my own house. You know anything about that?"

"No, man. I know nuthin' 'bout that. I can check 'round, yo, but I ain't heard so far."

"I appreciate it, Roberto. That gang bust last month is probably the place to start. Keep in touch."

Roberto Martinez became an undercover right-arm for Duncan some two years ago when the detective took down the gang that was threatening Roberto's father's bakery. Martinez senior refused to pay 'protection' money, so they were going to kill him.

Roberto knew of Duncan and called him at

work one day. After telling him the story, he begged the detective not to ignore him. He was so frightened for his father.

Duncan was not the 'can't help you 'til they break the law' kind of cop, and no one hated gangs more than he did. He set up the bakery with cameras and waited. When the time came all six members walked in with guns and he was ready for them. When it was all over, two were dead and four in long term prison sentences, and not a bit of damage to the bakery.

Roberto helped him out whenever he could since then. The last time was the gang members that shot the little boy. Seems thugs like to brag about their horrendous deeds. Duncan was glad to have Roberto on his team.

Duncan wanted to find out what was going on as fast as possible. This is his home he was talking about. No punk was going to get away with an attack so personal.

Back at Adriana's personal cell phone

numbers, he found several going to a Shane Abet. That name didn't ring a bell, but he pulled him up on the monitor anyway.

Seems our boy has multiple B&Es in his past and as well as some drug charges. Nothing like murder, that was a given, but you never know what will set people off.

Could Adriana have paid this dude to break-in his own home before her death? Roger doubted it, because he didn't have anything that she would want.

Whoever he is, this is a punk that needs to be seen face to face.

Chapter

13

Roger left the precinct and drove to the address Shane gave for his home. Turning west at the corner of E. Mt. Vernon and Oliver, he pulled into a home that was neat as a pen. He certainly wasn't expecting such a perfect little doll house for this low life felon.

When he knocked on the door, a small woman answered.

"Good afternoon, Ma'am. I am Detective Roger Duncan and I am looking for Shane Abet. Is he here?"

The woman asked him in. They both sat in a neat and tidy living room.

"Detective, Shane is my son and he is not here. Actually, he does not even live here. I am Dora Abet and this is my house. He has an apartment somewhere up in the Old Town area. He lives with his girlfriend, Shelli."

"When was the last time you saw your son, Mrs. Abet?"

"It has been several months, I'm afraid. He only comes around here when he needs something, and that is usually money. He gets into trouble and he thinks I am going to pay his attorney to keep him out of jail. I did for a while, but no more. I have run out of patience. He never seems to learn from his mistakes, and I can't help him anymore.

"If he has broken the law, and I assume he has or you wouldn't be here, then it's time he went to jail where he belongs.

"But it seems he is making enough money on his own right now that he doesn't need to come and ask for mine. That is always a good thing. I don't know how he is making it, and quite frankly, I don't want to know." She gave a small grin after that statement.

"What is Shelli's last name?"

"I have no idea, Detective Duncan. I only met her once. I can't say you will be impressed with her, though. She isn't very bright, if you get my drift. Not autistic exactly, but close. If Shane told her the sun was brown, she would believe it because she doesn't have the mental capacity to know any better. Poor thing.

"I have no idea what Shane sees in her, but then again, he isn't much of a catch either, with his ugly tattoos and piercings. Then add that to his life style decisions...." She wiped a tear from her eye and stared at the floor for a moment.

Roger knew he would have to start over to find this guy, but was glad to get the added information. It's tough for a mother to be honest like this. He wondered what it would feel like to know you have given life to a loser.

"Thank you, Ma'am. I am sorry to bother you, but I do appreciate your help." He handed her his card. "Please call me if you hear from him."

He left and drove back downtown. Old Town apartments were high priced. Only those with serious money can afford them. It was the trendy new thing for young professionals, not the Shane Abets of the world. A condo made out of the old downtown industrial buildings had a waiting list of high-end buyers. Duncan didn't understand the industrial look appeal, but to each his own.

When he returned to his desk, he did a search for apartments. There weren't all that many since most were turned into condos for sale.

The ones he did find were running about Twenty-five hundred to three thousand dollars a month. Where would a punk like Shane, get that kind of money? This just might be the guy he has been looking for.

Duncan's phone rang and when he answered, he was talking with the private investigator, Lana Carter. She agreed to meet with him to discuss Adriana. They agreed to meet at McDonald's for coffee at three this afternoon.

He took lunch about one-thirty and went to find an old friend of his, Dan Simms. He found him where he always did, in his garage workshop on the west side of the city.

Roger told Dan what he needed, gave him cash and a key, then headed east for his appointment with Ms. Carter.

When they met outside McDonald's on N. Broadway a little before three. Lana walked up to him and introduced herself. Seems the badge clipped to his pocket gave him away.

They purchased coffee and sat down.

"Lana, do you mind if I call you Lana?"

"Let's do this the easy way. You are Roger and I am Lana. Does that work for you?"

Roger liked this straightforward woman. She appeared to be in her mid-thirties, slender and tanned. Wichita summers will do that to you.

"Lana?"

"Yes."

"Heard about Adriana?"

"Yes. Clues?"

"None." They both laughed at their curt conversation.

"Well, what I need to know, Lana, is what kind of work you did for her."

"Well, I have to tell you, Roger, she was one of a kind. I never had a client that was so wrapped up in taking care of abandoned children in my life. She was wonderful."

Duncan choked on his coffee. "Are we talking about the same woman? Adriana Mason hated children!"

Lana's eyebrows went up. "Well, not the woman I knew. She hired me to find neglected children so she could help them out. You know, parents who let their children starve so they could use their money to buy drugs, stuff like that."

"How often did you do this for her?"

"She hired me about eight to ten times a year. I have to admit, she paid well, too."

Roger was dumbfounded. Here was a

woman who hated children. She wouldn't take the time to take care of her own niece, but would pay well to find neglected and unwanted children so she could help them? This can't be the same woman?

"How would you come up with this information?"

"Roger, I have a friend in Child Services. She calls me whenever a really difficult case comes up. You know, the ones where the parents are living off state money they get for the kids, but they spend it on junk for themselves.

"So many times the state's hands are tied and those kids are returned to worthless parents. I would go to where they lived and watch them for several days. I have to admit, there have been several days when I would bring food to feed kids that would be locked outside all day with nothing to eat or drink.

"I took pictures and would show Adriana. She would get so upset just seeing the photos!"

Lana stared at her now empty coffee cup.

"What would she do then?"

"I don't know really. I would give her the photos and info. She took it from there. Then I would send the bill and she paid it.

"There was one case that really got to me, though. I couldn't get that child out of my mind, so I revisited the little boy's house about two months after turning it over to her. Well, there were no more starving children locked outside! I went around and looked in windows. There were two adults stoned out of their minds, but not a child in the house. She obviously took care of it. I'm telling you, she was a saint."

"Did you do any other work for her?"

"Nope. That was it. She would call and tell me what my next assignment was. Sometimes she got specific, like, wanting me to find a Hispanic male child that was being abused, or she wanted me to find a black girl that was

167

neglected. She would get pretty specific at times."

"Lana, when was the last time you heard from her?" Duncan still couldn't picture this image of Adriana. She didn't care about anyone but herself.

"The last time I heard from her was about a month ago, Roger. She wanted me to find a blond Caucasian girl, about one or two years old. I worked on that for three weeks, but I am afraid I was unable to find one. I went over all of the cases that my friend could come up with and no one was mistreating or had abandoned a little blonde girl. Now brown or black hair, yes! I found several, but that didn't interest her."

"When you told her, what did she do?"

"She just said okay and hung up. That was it. I sent her a bill for my time and she paid it. That was my last contact with her. Next thing I know, her murder is in the paper. I had to be out of town or I would have been at her funeral."

"Well, I appreciate your help, Lana. I don't know why we haven't met before."

"To tell you the truth, Roger, I am surprised too. I know a lot of the detectives. Donna Decker is my favorite. Now there's a sweetheart."

The mention of his friend, Lou's, partner brought a smile to his face.

"Yes, she is. Her partner, Lou, is the envy of the squad!" They both laughed.

~~~

Roger Duncan's meeting with the private investigator was an interesting one. Lana told him Adriana was a saint and wanted to help abandoned children. But he knew better than that.

She just wanted to find children to sell that wouldn't be reported missing. What better way to do it? The druggy parents might not even know they were gone, and even if they did, they wouldn't report it because they would lose their state money.

Who knows. The way he saw it, she had a "client" who wanted a child, for whatever reason. If the client wanted a specific gender or color, or a specific look, that would be on the order, too.

She was into human trafficking of children. You don't get any lower than that. When Lana couldn't come up with a blonde girl, she stole her own niece.

Roger doubted she would get her own hands dirty, so there had to be someone who went and picked them up after Lana found them, and right now he was putting his money on that punk Abet, and maybe his brown-sun girlfriend.

He couldn't find any fault with Lana's actions. Nothing she did was illegal and she truly believed she was helping save those children's lives. The information at Child Services was public information, so her friend didn't break the law either. Lana reported abused children, thinking Adriana, being an attorney, would have them legally removed to save the children. She certainly had been fooled. But then again, he knew how good an actress that attorney could be.

The baby food found in her house has to mean she had babies there, so it was easy to conclude someone would pick up the child, get it to Adriana, and then she would take them home for whatever amount of time, before passing them onto the client. Probably to fatten them up if they had been too neglected.

Duncan's thoughts were bouncing off the walls. How long would that take? To get a malnourished child back healthy? Or abuse marks to heal? He knew it wasn't for the sake of the child that Adriana did it. To get the highest price for a kid, they had to look good.

Lana couldn't find her a blonde little girl. So Adriana found her own. Her sister's little girl was close enough and her sister was dying anyway, so why not?

The one thing she didn't seem to take into consideration was that Angelina would call the cops and want her child back. No one had done that before. She would have gotten away with it if she had just waited a little longer. When her sister died, Taylor could have disappeared and no one would have known anything about it.

As these thoughts rolled over and over again, the more ill he felt.

Adriana was one of the most evil people he had ever met.

Duncan headed straight for Parry's office. His boss looked surprised when Roger walked in, shut the door and sat down in front of his desk.

"I take it you want to talk to me?" The captain put down his pen and shut the folder he was working on.

"Yes, sir. I want to tell you a fairy tale about the wicked witch of Wichita and how she came to be known that way."

"Well, sounds like it's time for a break. Go ahead, Roger, enlighten me on how this fairy tale came into being…"

"Well, sir, once upon a time, there was a beautiful witch…"

Chapter

14

After explaining Adriana to Parry, his boss said he was going to get the D.A. on the phone for a chat. That was what Roger was hoping for. It wasn't a matter of ruining Adriana's reputation, she had done that herself. It was a matter of her illegal actions being brought out into the light.

Back at his desk, he pondered these facts when he got a call he was waiting for.

"Duncan, it's Roberto. Hey, man, there's a price on your head, yo."

"Really? Who's after me, Roberto?"

"I haven't found that out yet, but you better watch your back, dog, know what I mean? I hear the price is five-Gs. That would buy a lot of drugs, yo, so there may be a bunch of takers. I'll get back when I have more info. Gotta go." The phone clicked off.

Duncan stared at the phone for a few seconds before putting it down. A price on his head. Yep, the gang bangers were out for him. What was worse, that five thousand is exactly how much was missing from his house. His own money was paying for the hit on him.

Roger knocked on the captain's door again. This time to give him an update on himself. After the usual 'watch your back' comments, he went back to work.

Pulling the electric company's records, he found Shane Abet. As his mother said, he was renting an expensive Old Town apartment. The apartment phone was in his girlfriend's name, Shelli Harms.

Well, it was time to meet the scumbag face to face.

~~~

Shelli Harms ran her hand down the side of her skinny jeans, wondering if Shane liked the way she looked in them. She hoped so.

Abandoned as a child and raised in foster care, she didn't have many friends. But she didn't care because Shane Abet was her moon and stars, and she hoped someday he would make her his wife.

She will wait forever if she had to. No, she would wait even longer! She knew she wasn't as smart as he was, but Shane didn't seem to mind.

She didn't have to be smart, because Shane was. He made a lot of money working for that attorney lady.

Shelli thought she was a lawyer, but Shane said she was an attorney. That sounded even more important. Working for her meant they could live in such a nice place. None of her old friends would ever believe she had it so good.

Shane is worried now that the lady attorney is dead, but she knew something wonderful would come up. It always did.

Maybe they could go to Lake of the Ozarks on their honeymoon. She had never been there before! They had enough money since they picked up that blonde girl. That was the most money they ever made. Shane said they made ten-K, whatever that meant. But he said it was a lot so, of course, she believed him.

They were in Delano, parked a couple of

blocks away from a coffee shop. He told her to watch for that attorney. Shelli always did as she was told. She felt that's why they worked so well together. He figured out what needed to be done and she did what he told her to do.

Well, that woman came around the building with a kid. She sat her down on a bench, fed her something, and then left. Shane was so excited.

"Go! Go get the kid!" he said, giving Shelli a shove out of the van. She knew he didn't mean for her to trip and fall. He would have said he was sorry if he wasn't so wrapped up in his work. She got up off the ground and started walking.

She walked until she came right up on the little blonde girl. The child smiled up at her. Goodness, this kid was healthy. Not at all like the others.

"It's okay, princess. Want to take a little walk?" Shelli crooned.

She wondered how many children she and Shane would have some day. She hoped they had eight or ten and that they would all look like him. She loved his blue eyes. Not like her brown eyes. Shane said they were boring and, of course, he is always right. She is so lucky to have a guy like him to love her.

She walked the little girl back to the van and they drove away. The kid was lulled to sleep by the movement of the vehicle as they drove back through Wichita. She loved car rides. Especially with her Shane.

It took about a half hour to make it to the Vickridge housing district on the east side. Next to the circle driveway was a really huge home in one of the more upscale neighborhoods in the city.

Shane cut the engine and told her to wake the girl, so she did. Shane then walked her to the front door of the home.

This woman opened the door and called out,

"Randy! They're here!"

The woman and man took the girl into their enormous home, after handing a sealed envelope to Shane.

Well, that envelope held more money than she had ever seen in her entire life. She tried to count it but couldn't figure it out. Shane said it wasn't all for them, but he said some of it was. They went home and she took good care of him that night.

The next day he left and said he had to meet with the attorney and give her the money. When he came back, he brought a pizza and some cocaine. They had a wonderful time that night, too, from what she remembered.

Yeah, the lady attorney was dead now. Who would want to do that? She knew Shane was worried.

He was sleeping now, but when he woke up, she would make sure he enjoyed the rest of the afternoon. He preferred for her to be on top and that is exactly what she will do.

Someone was knocking on the door. Did he order another pizza?

~~~

Duncan took three officers with him to Abet's apartment. When a young woman opened the door, they stormed into the place and found Shane in the bedroom. The frightened girl was Shelli Harms.

After hauling them downtown, he couldn't wait to get into an interview room with each of them.

He started with the one he felt would be the easiest to swing, the girl. Like Shane's mother said, she really wasn't too bright.

When he walked into the interview room, Shelli looked scared. That's exactly how he wanted her to be.

182

"Can I see Shane? I need to see Shane!"

"No, you can't. The only one you will get to see is me. And if you don't answer my questions, I will make sure you never see Shane again." Duncan was in no mood for games. A child's life was at stake.

"What do you know about Adriana Mason?" Right to the point. His icy stare wasn't lost on her, either.

"The lady lawyer, uh, I mean attorney? I don't know anything."

"Yes, you do. You and your boyfriend worked for her, didn't you? You stole children for her, didn't you? You got paid to kidnap babies, didn't you?"

"No, I mean, yes. I mean… uh, yes. Well, we did pick up children for her. Yes, she paid us to do it." Shelli was flustered.

"You picked up a little blonde girl in Delano

183

a while back. Where is she?"

"Well, I don't…"

"*WHERE IS SHE?* Do you want to spend the rest of your sorry life in prison? If not, you had better tell me where she is!" Duncan was not going to be soft on this scum. He wanted Taylor back.

"I don't know why you are yelling at me. She went to a really nice home in Vickridge! What's wrong with that?" Shelli broke down and cried.

Duncan couldn't believe this woman didn't think there was anything wrong with kidnapping a young child. She put a new definition on stupid.

"Because there is a mother who is worried sick because her little girl has been kidnapped by you and your scumbag boyfriend! She wants her child back!"

"Where in Vickridge did you take her? I want an address. NOW!" His heart was pounding as his fist beat down on the table. Was he really going to find this little girl? Was Taylor even alive?

"I don't *know* the address. Shane was driving. He knew where to go." She was in complete hysterics by now.

Duncan got up and left the room. He didn't care if she cried, but he knew she wouldn't be able to give him any more information.

But it didn't take much to figure out who could and he headed right for that interview room.

Chapter

15

When he walked in, another detective was interviewing the boyfriend. Overlooking the detective's surprised glance, Roger grabbed Shane by the neck, pulled him off the chair and slammed him against the wall.

"Where in Vickridge did you take that little blonde girl? *WHERE?*"

The other detective knew better than to get

in the way when Duncan was like this. He hardly ever lost his temper, so when he did, everyone knew it was important. Since there was a child involved, it obviously was a very good reason. He just leaned against the wall with his arms crossed and watched.

"Help, someone, help me! He's going to kill me!" It was Shane screaming for help.

"You got that right, scumbag. You're dead meat unless you talk. Now, where is that child?"

Seeing that the other investigator was not going to come to his rescue, he said, "Okay, *okay.* Let me down."

Duncan threw him back on his chair, put a piece of paper and pen in front of him and growled, "Write. *NOW.*"

Shane knew he was caught, and he would bet Shelli spilled everything. He should have known better than to hang with someone so stupid. He never wanted to lay eyes on her again.

She was lousy in bed to boot, and she had the nerve to turn on him after all he did for her?

Not having a choice, Shane wrote down the address where the child was taken.

Duncan grabbed the paper and put it in his pocket.

"How many children did you kidnap for Adriana Mason? How many?"

Flustered, Shane said, "I don't know. A dozen. Two, maybe. I mean, they were just unwanted kids."

It was all Duncan could do to keep from knocking Shane's head off, so he turned to the other detective and said, "I am sure he remembers each and every one of them."

His comrade nodded in total agreement and Duncan left the room.

Calling for three squad cars to follow him, he informed the captain he knew where Taylor was. He got Parry's okay to take whatever action needed to get her out of there safely.

Vickridge was a newer area of Wichita where the ultra-rich lived. Homes started at a mil and went up. All he could think about was some rich pervert had bought himself a toy. By the time he arrived at the circle drive, he was crazy out of his mind and ready to kill.

All the officers were at the door with him except two who went around the back in case anyone felt like running.

He rang the doorbell which was opened immediately by a woman in a maid's uniform. He pushed his way in and saw a couple in the living room with Taylor sitting on the floor playing with some toys.

He ran for the child, grabbing her up as the officers restrained and handcuffed the man and woman with her, who were screaming and yelling.

The adults demanded to know who they thought they were, coming into their house like that. They promised to get every one of them fired. They screamed at him to put down their child. Duncan could care less what they said and yelled at the uniforms to get them out of his sight. He wanted them away from Taylor.

After they were removed from the house, Duncan gave Taylor to one of the officers and told him to put her in his squad and keep a close eye on her until he was done. He sent two uniforms to search the house for other occupants, while he questioned the maid.

The maid, who was crying because of all the commotion, was questioned about the home.

"No there weren't any more children in the house."

"No, no one else is in the house because the cook and gardener have already gone home."

"No, there never had been any other children

in the house that I know of. I have worked here for four years."

"Yes, the Wendalles adopted the little girl because they couldn't have any children of their own."

"No, I don't know anything about the adoption. They would never share that information with the hired help."

Roger left the maid with an officer to get her personal information before letting her go, as well as that of the other employees.

After the officers reported the house was safe, Roger Duncan decided to look around. He found a little girl's room fit for a queen. Well, at least she was treated well.

Thank you, God, for not letting this be what I thought it might be. At least they took good care of her.

When he was through at the house, he put

Taylor in his car, buckled her into the back seat and headed east. He called Parry with the latest update and they both were ecstatic Taylor was found, safe and sound.

Parry kept telling him what a great job he'd done. The captain was just a happy as Duncan.

It was all Roger Duncan could do to keep from staring at Taylor in the rearview mirror while he was driving her home. Though he wanted to seat her next to him, she was belted into the back seat as the law requires.

She seemed healthy, expensively dressed and appeared to be happy. She was carrying one of her dolls.

"See, my dolly?" She held up the doll for him to see.

"I see that! Wow. She sure is pretty. What's her name?" Looking in the mirror he could see her grin.

"Her name is Molly. Do you like her name?" The child was looking up at him with innocent eyes.

"Boy, I sure do. Molly is a great name, Taylor."

"Do I have to go to bed, now?" Her lip pushed out into a pout.

Laughing, Roger said, "No, not for a little while. I am going to take you to see your mommy! Would you like that?"

Tears came to her eyes and she spoke almost in a whisper, "Which mommy?"

Shocked, he didn't know what to say, but just blurted out, "Your only mommy!"

Her eyes got really big. "Yes, I want my mommy!" Then she started to cry. How he wanted to put his arm around her. Roger didn't blame her, he was about to cry also.

Pulling up to Angelina's apartment was one

of the happiest moments of his life. He did it. He found her child before she died.

After knocking on the door and waiting. The door slowing opened. When Angelina saw Taylor, and Taylor saw her mother, the tears became a typhoon. Even Roger let go of a few.

Angelina hugged him, then hugged Taylor, then hugged him again. All she could say was 'I love you' to Taylor. The child was just as glad to see her and came back with 'love you too, mommy.'

Taylor added, 'Where have you been, mommy? They said you were gone. Where did you go?'

After several moments of tears and hugs, Roger went outside to make a call.

When the captain answered again, he told him what was on his mind. He further said he would do whatever Parry told him to do to make it work.

Parry thought for a moment and then told him his plans to 'tie up all the loose ends in order to make his report complete' was perfectly within the job of a detective. His boss told him to do whatever it took to make it happen.

Duncan thanked him, then called his friend, Lou. After explaining the situation, Lou told him what he wanted to know.

Next, he called a woman he felt would like to hear what he had to say. Everything was falling into place.

When he re-entered the apartment some twenty minutes later, Taylor was asleep on Angelina's lap. Momma's eyes were still watering, but only in happiness. She pointed to the chair for him to sit.

"I can never thank you enough for what you have done. We both know I don't have but a short time left, but I don't care, now that I have Taylor with me."

"You will never know how much the pleasure is all mine. Finding Taylor had become my life's work. I shouldn't get so involved with a case, but I did here and I am not sorry. Meeting you, then Taylor, has been the highlight of my year." He almost said 'the highlight of my life,' which certainly would have been the truth.

She smiled a sad smile while rubbing Taylor's hair.

"I have to ask one more thing of you, if you will humor me." Duncan didn't want to push her if she was weak and couldn't handle it.

"Anything, Roger. I will do anything for you." He could see in her eyes she meant it.

"Okay, I want you and Taylor to be ready to leave the apartment tomorrow morning at 9 o'clock. Is that too early for you?"

"No. I think I can make it. Whatever for?"

"Oh, no. You can't ask questions, Angelina.

You just have to have faith."

They both laughed and she nodded her head yes. Knowing she was weaker than before, he carried Taylor to her bed so Angelina wouldn't have to. The child looked like an angel, asleep in her own little bed.

Roger told her to get some sleep so she would be rested for the morning.

"Oh, I will, but I am going to get my pillow and blanket and sleep right next to Taylor. I don't want her to be out of my sight again."

"You can't sleep on that hard floor!" Roger went into the other bedroom and grabbed the full-sized top mattress, linens and all. He maneuvered it into Taylor's room and laid it on the floor.

"There, now you can be comfortable!" He smiled wide. He actually felt like the proverbial white knight!

"Oh, how wonderful. That's perfect!"

She walked him to the door. He bent down and kissed her forehead and shut the door behind him.

When he left, there was an errand he had to make before heading home. After getting everything arranged for the morning, he made a couple of phone calls and everything was set.

Once in bed, he said a prayer of thanks for how well the day came out and then he fell soundly asleep for the first time in months.

Chapter

16

The next morning found Roger awake at six. He just couldn't sleep any longer. He showered, dressed, had breakfast and was ready to go by seven.

That's when he called Bob Boyce, of Boyce's Moving Service, and made a special request. As Lou predicted, Bob said yes without hesitation.

Roger was as excited as a kid. He didn't think he could wait, but eight-thirty finally came around and he headed for Angelina's for their nine o'clock appointment.

When he arrived, she opened the door without his knocking. She was dressed to the teeth and was wearing makeup and her wig.

Wow. All Roger could think of was her beauty. Then Taylor came around the corner in a soft lacy dress that just melted his heart. After telling them how beautiful they both were, he asked Angelina for her keys. All of them. She really looked concerned now, but didn't hesitate to do what he asked.

She had questions in her eyes, but all he would do was usher them both to his car.

"No questions, my ladies. Into your chariot, please." Playing the knight in shining armor again made him feel good. Really good. Today was going to be the best one he could ever remember.

Another fifteen minutes and they were in the middle of Eastborough, where the homes were large and regal. He pulled into the driveway of Adriana's house and stopped.

He went around to open the car door for the two ladies and used the sweep of his arm to point them to the front door.

"What are we doing here? Roger, what is going on?" She really looked worried now.

He did not say a word, only escorted her and Taylor to the front steps.

When they made it to the door, it flew open and there stood Carol Parker, the housekeeper, "Welcome home!" Roger was glad she found the keys he had left for her on the front porch the night before.

Angelina looked at him with concern but he just kept making her walk on into the home.

She leaned over to him and asked, "What is

going on? You know I don't live here."

"Oh yes you do, Madam," he said with a big smile.

He explained to her that she did indeed live here now. It was her sister's place and since there was no other family, she inherited it. She and Taylor also had Carol as their housekeeper, cook, and babysitter, when needed. She would be living on the property 24/7.

Angelina stood with her mouth open as she looked around.

"Adriana lived *here?*" Angelina couldn't believe it.

Carol leaned to Roger and said, "You were right! She is the spitting image of Adriana!" His comment back was to assure her she would love the difference between the two.

Turning to Taylor, Carol said, "Taylor, would you like some chocolate pudding?" When

Taylor giggled and said yes, they both went into the kitchen while Roger and Angelina stayed in the living room.

There was a knock on the door. Duncan jumped to open it.

"Hey, you must be Roger. I'm Bob Boyce. We have your stuff, so I hope we are not too early."

"Right on time, my friend. Right on time. Bring it on in and put it right down that hall, first door on the right is the first-floor master."

Bob and two other guys started carrying in a few boxes and a couple of wardrobes. Duncan explained to Angelina that when they left the tiny furnished apartment she had been forced to live in, he left her keys under the mat.

Bob and his crew went in and packed up all of her personal clothes and items that she would want. They were being delivered to her new home. They would never have to go back there again. Bob even drove her car to her new place.

"Uh, and I told your old landlord you were moving out today and wouldn't be back." Roger was enjoying the look of wonder all over her face.

He told her he would be right back and stepped out on the front porch and shut the door behind him. He was standing there alone with Boyce. Roger thanked him for doing this with absolutely no advanced warning and asked what he owed for the move.

"Steak and potatoes."

Roger thought he misunderstood and said, "Excuse me?"

"Steak and potatoes. That's the cost of this little move. Look, Lou called me last night and told me what was going on and why you were doing this, so I was not surprised when you called this morning. I already had a crew ready to get it done in a hurry.

"Detective, she didn't have much of anything. Didn't take long to empty that tiny place out. Of course, we had to put a mattress back on the bed, but that was nothing. For heaven's sakes, we were in and out of there in less than thirty minutes!

"But to answer your question, there is absolutely no charge. Thanks for letting me help. But, my wife and I never turn down a good bar-b-q, so the next time you decide to cook steak and potatoes…" Bob was grinning ear to ear.

"You've got it, my friend. I won't forget!" Roger shook Bob's hand and watched him leave.

After the movers left, Roger went back inside to a teary eyed Angelina.

"I think I have said this before, but how will I ever repay you…"

"I have been paid back with your smile. That's all I want."

She leaned up on her tip toes and kissed him on the mouth. Now it was his mouth that fell open.

After being shown around, the first-floor master bedroom was perfect for her and Taylor. She wouldn't have to climb the stairs and the wheelchair would even fit into the bathroom, if needed. Normally reserved for guests, Adriana had used the master upstairs.

Roger's trip here last night paid off,. He was able to hide the keys for Carol outside and add a twin bed to the master bedroom, surrounded with toys for a little girl. He knew Angelina would want her in the same room.

There was no reason why Taylor couldn't be with her mom.

Her only mom.

~~~

The rest of his day was spent at his desk doing just what Parry had suggested. Adding the morning's activities to the ending of his report would make it finished.

From detecting a large number of phone calls to Shane Abet; to finding and arresting him and his girlfriend; to getting Shane to admit to the kidnapping ring and the location of the missing child, Taylor Jenkins.

From there, his report goes to the return of the unharmed child to her lawful mother; then the moving of child and mother to a safer neighborhood, which the mother had inherited from the kidnapper.

After getting the report altogether, he read it over one last time.

Who would believe this story, Lord? The one who did the vilest of crimes is the one that made the victims wealthy and able to live in a safer environment than they had before. Who would believe that? Your justice is perfect, Lord, as usual.

Roger finished his report, shut down his computer and headed for home. It had, indeed, been a good day.

Chapter

17

"STOP IT! JUST STOP IT!"

Duncan had answered his phone and someone was yelling at him.

"Who *is* this?"

"You *know* who this is! Get those thugs off my tail. I haven't done anything illegal and I did not kill Adriana. I *wanted* to, but I didn't!"

Duncan then recognized the voice. It was Derrick Porter. *Guess he doesn't like being tailed by the police.*

"My clients are getting antsy and I don't blame them. Are you trying to put me out of business?" He seemed to be coming unglued.

"No, Mr. Porter. I just need to know what you're hiding, and you *are* hiding something." *Good job, Duncan. Straight to the point.*

Silence.

Then in a much calmer voice, Porter gave a heavy sigh, then said, "Look we need to meet. You want to know everything? I'll tell you everything. Just say when and where."

Duncan knew it had to be somewhere they could be in private and not be recognized. That could cause a media stir after last year's problems.

"Crooked attorney meets with WPD

detective! Which one is on the take?"

"Crooked attorney may be under investigation again!"

"Wichita detective trying to make a deal?"

It really wasn't funny, but he had to restrain a chuckle.

"I assume you know where Adriana lived?"

"Uh, yeah. I was there once for a party. Eastborough, right?"

"Yeah." Duncan gave him the address and told him to meet him there at six tonight. "We can talk without the media being all over us."

"That's creepy, detective, but I'll be there."

As soon as he hung up, he called Angelina. The last time he saw her was two days ago when he moved her. He told her of his situation and asked if he could have the meeting with Porter there since there was a very nice den that could

213

be closed off for a private talk. She readily agreed.

He wasn't about to overlook Porter's mistake. In his emotional state, he said he didn't kill her, *but he wanted to*. Doesn't sound like the happy 'friends and colleagues' that he had painted them out to be. So he really did want her dead….

~~~

Duncan arrived a few minutes early and found Angelina sitting in a new electric wheelchair, looking lovely. He was amazed at how happy and well, healthy, she looked.

"Good evening, Detective Duncan!" She smiled as she let him in.

"I thought we had agreed on Roger."

"Oh yes, indeed. How silly of me. Good evening, Detective Roger!"

He was loving her kidding and relished in her looking so good. It was impossible to tell her wig wasn't the real thing. How beautiful can someone get?

She led him to the den, furnished with the finest white leather furniture he had ever seen. Two couches faced each other and on the table between them was a bottle of high-end white wine.

Roger smiled and said, *"Niiiice."*

She smiled back and showed him another bottle at the end of the room where a wet bar was located.

"Angelina, you look wonderful. And I must say, I love your electric wheel chair. Very nice!"

"Well, when you have so much money, you might as well spend it on things to make life easier." She smiled at him and his heart skipped a beat.

He sat down on one of the couches just as the doorbell rang.

Angelina told him to stay seated, and she would bring Mr. Porter in. She then moved her electric wheelchair out of the room.

A moment later he heard her yell, *"ROGER! Help!"*

Fear jabbed his veins! What was going on? Did the gang members follow him here? Did they have a gun on Angelina? He couldn't move fast enough as he flew to the front door.

While in route, she heard Taylor yell, "What's wrong, Mommy?"

Arriving at the front door, he stopped. He stared at the scene in front of him. Angelina was sitting in her chair staring at the man on the floor. Taylor was staring at her mother and holding her hand. Carol was kneeling down over the man.

Then there was the man, himself. Derrick Porter. Passed out. Face down. On the floor.

"Uh, I... uh, I just opened the door! He looked at me and then... well, he just fell down!" Angelina didn't know what was happening or why.

Roger's fear and adrenaline rush turned to laughter and he lost it. He threw his head back and laughed until the tears came.

Angelina and Carol looked at him like he was having a breakdown. He thought they may be right. He was sure it was the funniest thing he had ever seen!

When he could finally control himself enough to speak, he dried his eyes and said, "Oh, my. Oh, my. Uh, I uh... I guess I forgot to tell him about *you.* I'll bet he thought you were a ghost!"

That brought laughter from the two women as Carol helped Roger get the man to the couch.

She then went to the kitchen for some water.

When Derrick came around and was able to set up, he drank some of the water and then he saw Angelina again.

Roger jumped in quickly, "She is not Adriana. This is her *sister*, Angelina. Her *twin* sister. Her *identical* twin sister! She lives here now with her daughter Taylor, who is staring at you from behind Angelina."

"Uh…, how do you do, Ange… Angelina? I'm a bit embarrassed by my reaction, but outside of the chair, you are, indeed, identical."

When the chuckles and apologies were over, Roger led Derrick into the den and shut the double French doors behind him. The last he saw was Angelina smiling at him. He winked back.

Roger poured them both a glass of wine and sat on the opposite couch, facing Derrick.

Derrick took a sip, then started.

"Identical twin sister, detective? You have *got* to be kidding. I would *never*....

"Well, anyway, I certainly wasn't expecting such a nice reception." He lifted his glass of wine in acknowledgment.

Roger didn't want to spend the time socializing so he got to the point. "The nice reception, as you put it, was arranged by Angelina, not me."

Shaking his head he had to comment one more time, "She *is* identical. I just can't believe it. Adriana had a twin, an identical twin and she never told anyone."

"Well, one of the reasons may have been because her sister is the sweetest, kindest woman in the world, something Adriana knew nothing about. They were identical in looks only. Now, let's talk about the dead sister."

Derrick sipped his wine and stared at the floor. When he looked back up, he gave a small smile.

"Adriana and I did not get along at all, after we parted ways romantically. I can't say we did before, either, I just tolerated what she said and did, for the obvious sexual reasons. Plus, having her on your arm when you walked in somewhere, was a huge ego building trip. Every man in the place looked at me with envy. Turned out to be too big a price to pay.

"She was arrogant and self-centered. I am sure you already know that much. But what scared me the most is how she thought she could do anything and no one would care, even if it was illegal! Whatever she felt like doing was no problem to her. If it was what she wanted, that was all that mattered to her."

He was quiet for a moment, then went on, "It was Adriana who bribed that juror, not me. We stood to make a ton of money if things went our way, but she apparently didn't want to take that chance.

"By the time I found out about it, the media had me pegged for it. Seems she had some man call the juror, so he and everyone else just assumed it was me. The good news is, he could not pick out my voice as the one he talked to on the phone. That is really the only thing that saved me... reasonable doubt.

"If I had told the truth, it would have destroyed our law firm as well as appearing to just pass the buck, onto a gorgeous and popular attorney at that. I knew I couldn't compete.

"So, I just had to ride it out, and I did. Since I didn't do it, I figured they wouldn't find any evidence to convict me, and they didn't. But then there is the damaged reputation I get to live with for the rest of my life.

"We argued about it more than once. I would get angry and threaten to ruin her, and so on. I never did anything, but it wasn't because I didn't think about it.

"That day you came to my office and

mentioned kidnapping children, it was all I could do to keep from getting ill. It was the first I had heard about it, but I knew... I knew in my heart it was true. She would do anything for a buck. Stealing kids? No big deal!" He took a deep breath before continuing.

"After you left my office that day, I went home and got drunk for the first time in years. I was outraged. She was already dead, but I wanted to dig her up and kill her myself!

"I don't care if you believe me or not, but my lifestyle has been bought and paid for by my talents in the courtroom. I am good at what I do, detective. I would never do anything illegal that would jeopardize my entire life. And Adriana just about took everything away from me—including my freedom."

Derrick stopped talking and downed what was left in his glass.

Roger watched him in silence for a moment then said, "That certainly gives you reason to kill her."

"Yes, it certainly did, but I didn't do it. I am quite sure there are dozens of others who felt the same as I did. We both know I am not the only person she must have screwed to get what she wanted."

"Derrick, Adriana had lunch with the Mayor on a regular basis, and she told him she wanted you out of the firm after your shameful act with the juror, but you refused to leave."

"Well, that was a lie. It was just the opposite! I *did* want out. Big time! Anything to get away from her. She threatened me. She said she would go to the press and tell them she knew all about my jury tampering if I tried to leave the firm. I was bringing in a lot of money from my clients and she didn't want to lose that.

"Yes, detective, one of the best things that has ever happened to me was when someone put a bullet in that witches brain. Since then, I have actually slept well at night, and that is something

I had not been able to do since I met that woman."

Roger added, "She also told the Mayor she was afraid of you. Why do you think she said that?"

Derrick looked shocked and then became quiet. A couple of minutes passed before he spoke, but the sadness on his face was real.

"Don't you see, she was setting me up. If I had walked into her office one night and she shot me to death, she would have our popular and beloved mayor saying it had to be self-defense because he knew of her fear.

"Which brings me to this paperwork I brought to show you." Derrick took the papers out of his pocket and handed them across to Roger.

After looking them over, Duncan said, "Okay. This is a life insurance policy. What about it?

"Check the names. My secretary found this two days after her funeral when I finally got around to cleaning out her office. I paid Brenda extra to stay late with me and help out. Adriana had clients and I knew I would have to touch base with each of them and see if they wanted to retain a new attorney, or if they wanted me to handle their affairs. A major hassle, but that's the way it is.

"Anyway, it was in one of the locked drawers of her desk. It is a life insurance policy on *me*, for five million dollars. Of course, she is the beneficiary. I have no doubt in my mind that she was planning on collecting that money."

"Derrick, it's not unusual to have life insurance policies on partners in the same company. Companies take a financial hit when they lose one of their breadwinners."

"You are so right, but there was not one on her. And I was not *aware* of the one on me! She was just biding her time until she felt she needed more money, then I would have been the one shot to death!"

"Okay, Derrick, you have my attention." He poured them both another glass of wine. "But isn't that just another reason to want her dead?"

"It certainly would be, if I had known about it. But I didn't know about it until after her death. And besides, why wouldn't I have a policy on *her* if I was going to blow *her* away?"

Roger thought about that for a moment and had to agree. Plus, that was the third time Derrick referenced her death as 'being shot.' Granted, the newspaper didn't say how she died, only that she was murdered in her own home. Could it actually be that this man had nothing to do with Adriana's death? He was beginning to believe him.

If all he said was true, he was just another victim of one evil woman. If she would sell her niece away from her only sister, selling out her law partner would be no big deal. Roger knew there had to be many more victims.

Derrick was now up and walking the floor, while he remained seated, buried in all he had just heard. The truth was settling in on him.

Derrick Porter wasn't the crook Adriana made him out to be. He was just going to be another victim. And apparently, she wanted this victim to be dead. This, of course, would be much to her financial advantage. And financial advantage is what she wanted most in life.

Chapter

18

It was almost nine when Derrick left Angelina's home. She had let Taylor stay up because the child wanted Roger to tuck her in, which he was happy to do.

"Will you read me a story?"

"I will next time, how's that, little princess?"

"Okay. Give me a hug and kiss goodnight."

Roger was thrilled and thought his heart would stop when she put her little arms around his neck. As he left the room, he said good night and turned off the light.

Back in the living room with Angelina, he sat down for a few minutes to see how she was doing.

"I actually feel better than I have in a long while. Some of the effects of the chemo are wearing off. It is also the lack of financial stress and having such a nice place for Taylor to live. All thanks to you, of course."

Roger just stared at her for a moment, then opened his heart.

"Angelina, I know you have to be aware of this, so I might as well come out and tell you. I am in love with you. No doubt about it. It breaks my heart what you are going through, but I know there is nothing I can do about it. And Taylor has my heart too. I have known this for some time.

"I have never been able to find the woman of my dreams. I am forty-one and have never been married. I wanted real love, not some cheap imitation. For a lifetime type love. I feel that for you. Just thought you should know.

"I know you must worry about what will happen to Taylor when you are gone. I want you to know that I want to adopt her. I love her and will raise her as my own, and I will make sure she is always aware of her beautiful mother and what she was like.

"I know you have some really important things on your plate and you don't need my complicating things, but I hope you will forgive me.

Silence. Roger thought his heart would stop.

Angelina just looked at him for several minutes, before answering.

"Roger, you know you can't adopt Taylor. I mean, think about it. You are a single man who

231

carries a gun and works sixteen hour days when it's needed. No relatives that can take the place of a mother figure. See what I mean? The court would never give you Taylor."

He was stunned. The silence gave him time to digest what she said. Angelina was right. No one would let him have Taylor. Was it even right to want Taylor when he did work odd hours sometimes? It never occurred to him he couldn't be a good father.

As if reading his mind, Angelina said, "I am not saying you wouldn't be a good father, because I think you would be the best Taylor could ever hope for. I am just telling you to look at this logically. I don't see how it could possibly happen."

The subject of Taylor was dropped, but they talked a while longer. He told her of his opinion of Derrick, who was just another victim. They exchange thoughts about other victims until she showed signs of fatigue, then he left.

All the way home he was hurting. He could no longer think of his world without Angelina and Taylor! Adopting Taylor was the only way he knew of to keep them both in his heart. He could hardly breathe at the thought of Taylor going into the system.

~~~

Adriana and her crimes continued to dominate his mind. Taylor was safe, but there were still the ones who 'bought' her to deal with. They were wealthy and Roger knew sometimes that could make the difference between jail time and a slap on the wrist.

The next day he knocked on Captain Parry's door.

"Enter."

"Captain, what do you know about the couple that bought Taylor? What's going to happen to them?"

"Sit down, Duncan. The Wendalles? They will not be getting off easy. The DA is appalled by this whole Adriana thing. He intends to prosecute everyone involved to the fullest extent of the law. Child trafficking is a serious offense and the people that do the purchasing are just as guilty as those who do the selling.

"Plus, Adriana Mason's every move for the past five years is being heavily investigated. I am sure they will find more than we already know about." Parry just shook his head.

"I get it when people want to adopt, but with that kind of money, they could have done so legally and not had this problem." Roger really didn't get it. Why risk everything when it could have been done legally.

He was immediately brought back to the fact that he would probably not be able to adopt Taylor. At least not legally. That made him feel uncomfortable.

"Well, a lot of people wait on an adoption

list for years before a child comes along. I guess they just got tired of waiting. Anyway, the DA is going to make sure the newspaper has it on the front page for the next several months, so that others contemplating the same thing will think again.

"Plus, they are arresting the other couples that purchased kids from Adriana. Granted the children will go into foster care, but the purchasers will be prosecuted. At least the ones they can find. Seems Shane couldn't remember where half of them were dropped off. And some may have moved away. Who knows?

"But the Wendalles will definitely do time for their part in this. I doubt they will be able to afford to live in Vickridge again, once they get out." Parry seemed to enjoy the thought they probably would not be wealthy enough again to buy another human being.

"So, how are we coming on finding Adriana's killer?" Parry was looking right at him now.

"No closer than day one. I kid you not. We have solved a lot of stuff in the meantime, but not that one. She had so many enemies, it could be anyone of hundreds, thousands maybe." Duncan did not really care if he did find her killer. He would probably give the guy a medal if he did find him.

"Not good enough, Duncan. Start over, look at everything again. There is a killer out there and we need to find him. This Sunflower thing is driving me crazy."

"Yes, sir." Duncan left and went back to his desk.

The captain was right. I need to start over and look at everything with new eyes. There has to be something I missed. Sleazeball or not, Adriana was murdered and her killer needs to be caught. I agree with Parry. This Sunflower killer needs to be in jail.

The rest of the day he opened one folder after another. He needed to know what Adriana did from the time he talked to her until the day she died.

A call to her secretary, Betty Blackburn, gave him an idea of her work days and what time she left for home each evening. But what happened then? Was it one of her clients or was it something she did at night that got her killed. For all he knew, it could be one of her neighbors.

The thing he had to keep in mind is that he didn't plan to kill her. They used Adriana's own knife to stab her to death, so he didn't come prepared for a killing. Someone went to see her and ended up getting into an argument that caused her death. It was someone she apparently knew who was taller than she, which at five-foot-two, that would include about everyone.

That brought him back to Porter, but he no longer believed the man had anything to do with it. Oh, he certainly had a lot of reasons to do it, but Duncan knew in his gut he wasn't involved.

Adriana had almost destroyed him like she almost destroyed her sister. But Porter managed to work through it and not come unglued. Duncan was not so sure he could have overlooked her actions.

Good for you, Porter. How many others, Lord, how many others did she hurt or ruin?

His friend, Lou McGregor, walked up to his desk.

"Hey, we are going for some lunch. Wanna come along?"

When Roger looked up, he also saw Captain Parry walking toward him.

"Sounds like a good idea, Duncan. Get out of here and get some fresh air. This paperwork will still be here when you get back." Parry kept walking until he entered the break room. Duncan watched him pour another cup of coffee. The man lived on caffeine. But he couldn't fault his boss because there were some days he did, too.

Turning back to his friend, Roger said, "Sounds great, but not right now. I have a few things to tie up before I go. But I will take you up on that another time, my friend."

"Deal. Next time." Lou walked out with his partner and a co-worker Detective Jim Palmer.

Roger was getting hungry, but there was something he had to do first. He needed to write down a list of thoughts while they were fresh in his mind. Making notes helped him organize his thoughts.

For the next ten to fifteen minutes, he wrote down his thoughts in a fury. He didn't even stop to cross the ts. Once done, he turned his thoughts to food.

What would I like for lunch? Is it worth going out, or just ordering something in? He got up and stretched the stiffness from his back.

BOOOOMMMMMMM....!

Duncan jumped backward! What was *that?* It sounded like an explosion! But where? It didn't sound close, but it was close. *Wasn't it?*

Everyone in the room was running around, elbowing each other for space at the windows, trying to see something and asking each other questions.

Parry came out of his office and told everyone to settle down.

"We don't know what has happened, so we will NOT panic. Got that? As soon as I know something, I'll let *you* know. Now get back to work." He returned to his office.

The talk became hushed while everyone speculated on the cause of the explosion. Since their building was not falling down, they ruled out an inside bomb.

They all chatted about possibilities. If the

target wasn't the Wichita Police Department, could it have been the Sedgwick County Jail across the street? Or the Sedgwick County Courthouse next to the jail? Speculation involved every government building within a half-mile.

Ten minutes later, everyone heard the captain's phone ringing. Once again, time passed in silence.

Maybe the explosion wasn't a bomb. Could it have been an airplane that crashed? Terrorists? Who was the target? Did people die? The ideas were rampant as they waited to hear what was going on.

Outside, they could hear the fire department vehicles arriving with sirens blaring. They also knew the media would not be far behind. It was deadly quiet as everyone waited for the captain to inform them of what he knew.

When Parry hung up and came out of his office, he was pale as a ghost. Silence reigned.

"Nothing to worry about folks. It was a car bomb. There will not be a repeat. Get back to work. Duncan, in my office." Parry returned to his desk.

All of the other detectives and assistants stared at Roger as he walked into the captain's office. He had no clue what this could be about.

"Shut the door." Parry's voice was barely a whisper.

"What the…?"

"Just sit down, Roger." Parry was also sitting. "That car bomb we all heard? It was your car."

"My *WHAT?*" Duncan's eyes were like saucers. His mind was in overdrive trying to comprehend what is going on.

"Someone blew up your vehicle. A man getting into his car two slots down has been injured, apparently shrapnel hit him in the back.

He is on his way to the hospital. We won't know anything about his condition until later.

"Now, we have a pretty good idea who it was, don't we. You have a price on your head. The guy that called me was a member of the bomb squad. He told me it was a timed device.

"Apparently not high-end. Just your average, street thug type bomb. Instructions you can get off the internet. If you had gone to lunch, you would have been in it." The irony wasn't lost on either one of them.

"Wow. Guess someone was trying to collect some drug money."

"Roger, I think you need to lay low until this thing blows over. Maybe take some vacation time, whatever. I will have the guys look into it."

"Not going to happen, captain. I understand, and appreciate your concern, but my running away is not going to make the problem go away. We both know that." Duncan didn't have any answers at this time, but he sure wasn't going to let these thugs intimidate him any longer.

"There's one more thing. We don't know if it has anything to do with the bombing, but pieces of a Sunflower was found among the debris. Now don't go getting all charged up! We don't know if it came from your car or *what!*"

Roger choked on this news. "You are kidding me?" His mind racing to put pieces together that didn't fit.

Parry jumped back in, "We have no idea if it was a part of this or not. You know anything could have been blown around that site! For now, there is no linking the two.

"I will arrange for the city to provide you with a fleet car until you can settle up with your insurance company. I'll get one sent right over. That's about all I can do at this time."

"I appreciate that." Duncan was exhausted and his voice betrayed it.

Chapter

19

When Roger got home that evening, he noticed two squads watching his place, one on each end of the street. He wasn't going to argue this time.

Would they try and blow up my house? I guess they would if they thought I was in it. It wouldn't do much good if I wasn't here.

He pulled the car into his driveway and

immediately behind him was the bomb squad. They wouldn't let him go in without checking the place first. What he would normally consider a waste of time, was now greatly appreciated.

When they finished and found no explosives, he thanked them profusely. At least he could go to sleep thinking he had a chance of waking up. In the morning, he needed to check on his friend's technology.

Three messages from Angelina were on his answering machine. The bombing was on the news and she was desperate to talk to him. He couldn't think of anyone he would rather talk to.

After assuring her he was fine, they talked about Taylor and her day. She was going to be four in November, just three months away, and she wanted to learn to read for her birthday. What child would want that as a present? She was so special. Roger was so proud of her you would think he really was her father.

Angelina also told him she was getting some

of her papers in order so when the time came of her passing, there wouldn't be any problems. Roger didn't want to hear about that, but he didn't interrupt. By the time they said good night, his heart hurt.

~~~

Roger awoke early. After getting ready for work, he made his way up to the attic. His friend, Dan Simms, installed cameras and recording devices. Per Roger's instructions, there were two in the front of the house and one in the back. It was necessary after his house was broken into. Now, since his car exploded, it may end up being a lifesaver.

He went over the past week of digital tapes to no avail. Roger was relieved no one had tried to break in again. At least not yet. He reset the system, feeling grateful to have it in place.

He was able to read the morning newspaper while having a bite to eat. The front page pictured Roger and his bombed out car. He didn't like it, but at least Angelina won't be afraid when she sees it.

But the news wasn't all bad. The one thing that caught his eye further in the paper was the Engagement announcement of Kristina Peterson and Dr. Mark Weston.

Wow. He was really happy for her. Kristina deserved all the nice things she wanted in her life and she finally found a guy who could give them to her. He was glad for some good news in his life, for a change.

He tore out the announcement to go over again later and threw out the rest of the paper. It was time to get to work.

"How are you doing today?" It was the captain. As soon as he walked into the department, Parry came up to him.

"Good, really good. I got a great night's sleep, thanks to your forward thinking of the bomb squad. I noticed in this morning's paper, however, my face and name is splattered all over." Roger didn't like publicity.

"Come in and sit down."

Roger followed him into his office and grabbed a chair.

"Any more info on the Sunflower?" Duncan couldn't get a connection at all.

"No. Probably just a coincidence. Since all that happened yesterday afternoon, I forgot to give you some information I thought you might want to know. As it turns out, it was just as well I forgot, as more news came in this morning.

"Your baby stealing scumbag, Shane? He's dead. Seems some other prisoners didn't take well to his choice of profession. I really don't want to make light of this, because from what I was told, it was truly gruesome. He was gang raped, beaten, stabbed and left to bleed to death. Doc K says he had to have been in a great deal of pain while he bled out."

"I am not sure I am sorry for…."

"Let me finish," Parry interrupted. "News travels fast in the cell blocks as you already know. This morning, they found Shelli Harms dead. She had slit her wrists and bled out last night in her cell.

"Her cell mate didn't even know what she had done. Seems she went to bed with her makeshift tool, slashed herself, without uttering a sound, and laid there. She left a note under her pillow saying she couldn't live without her Shane. No one knows for sure if she did it because they would be apart in prison, or if she had heard he was dead. No way to know, but either way, she's gone, too."

Parry stopped talking and they both sat quietly with their own thoughts.

What makes people do such stupid things like kidnapping? Why would anyone want to live like that? How can you destroy people lives and not care? These people were low-lifes, no doubt, but even they shouldn't have ended up this way. Or should they?

Roger wasn't going to try and figure it out. What was done, was done.

He spoke quietly, "Anything else, captain?"

"Yes, a bit of good news. The man who was hit in the back by pieces of your car exploding is going to make it. Healing will take some time, but he will live."

Roger smiled and gave a thumbs up. Then he got up and left Parry's office.

At his desk, he mulled over the deaths he had just been told about. He felt bad about his own lack of remorse, but he didn't see any harm in them being gone. Those two caused so much pain to others, what's wrong with their feeling pain, too? *An eye for an eye, Lord?*

251

After a few moments of wondering how Angelina was doing, he turned back to his investigation and started thinking through each step.

Step one, Taylor is missing, but not from a day care center. He had successfully eliminated Kansas Kidz Center from the investigation.

Roger recalled the hugs and tears he got when he stopped by the center to let Doris McKenzie know her business will not be mentioned in the investigation. The report merely mentions that Adriana Mason falsely claimed to have dropped Taylor off at a daycare facility. That's it. There wasn't any reason to let Mason get away with hurting any more people.

Angelina was a caring mother who reported her child missing. Her sister jumped the gun, sold her too soon, and that alone got her caught.

Roger was horrified at the thought of what would have gone on if she had just waited until her sister had died. No one would have been the wiser and the child trafficking would have gone on forever.

Would Porter be alive? Probably not. Five million dollars was a lot of money to entice a murder. She had it all setup. Porter was right about her comments to the Mayor. He would have backed her up as having killed her partner in self-defense, and that is all she would have needed to walk off with the money.

Adriana had to have made many enemies. There had to be dozens out there that wanted her dead. Did another mother find out what happened to her child? Or even a father?

Going through the employee interviews again, he worked on the fake name Adriana wanted the janitor to use. She was obviously setting him up for some kind of fall. If she had lived, the janitor would probably be in prison for something he didn't do. Mind boggling.

There is no doubt in my mind about that. If she got caught, she probably was going to throw out the new name as the villain, and of course, it would come back to Lester. What a genius manipulator she was! Such evil behind such beauty.

"Duncan! In my office."

Now what? His life seemed to be spinning out of control.

"Yes, captain." Roger sat down before being told to. Just then his cell rang.

Holding up a finger, the captain nodded for him to take the call. He really wanted to take it because it was from Roberto, his underground friend.

"Yo, dog, no gang is after your butt. No kidding. Oh, they laughed when they saw what had happened to your car in the papers, but it weren't them, bro!

"Knowing that helps, yo. I'll be able to find out who put the bucks on you, since it wasn't the brothers. Gimme a couple of days."

"Thanks. I appreciate it." Roger hung up then gave the captain a rundown on this new information.

Parry was concerned, even angry. "If it isn't the gang, then who the *hell* wants you dead?"

"I don't know, but we will know when the person who put the money up is found. Plus, that person will also be the guy who broke into my house and stole the money in the *first* place."

"Well, the news just gets better and better, Roger. The reason I called you in here is because Rocky's been shot."

"What are you talking about? Rocky isn't even here…"

"No, he isn't. He was shot in Portland, Oregon, by an unknown assailant. He is in the hospital and we don't know his condition yet.

"He was shopping with his dad at a mall and

255

when they were getting into their car in the parking lot, a bullet hit him in the back. No one knows why. We don't know if the bullet was meant for him or if it was a random shooting. *NOTHING* is known right now!"

Parry slammed his fist on the desk. Seems too many of his detectives were being targets and he didn't like it one bit. First Duncan, now Rocky! The man is on vacation, for Chrissake!

"When are you supposed to hear something?" Roger couldn't believe it. He couldn't get to Rocky and he felt helpless. How does a detective face all the trials of the job and doesn't get shot until he goes to visit his father? He didn't want to lose his friend and partner.

"When he gets out of surgery."

Roger went back to his desk. He felt like he was breaking down. Everything is falling apart.

My partner is struggling for his life; the woman who has my heart is dying a painful death; I can't raise the little girl that I love because I won't be able to adopt her, and someone wants me dead, too! Could things get any worse, Lord?

If his heart wasn't aching enough, there's his job. This case of his, the one he said he could handle himself, is as cold as the day he got it.

There was no word about Rocky before Roger left at the end of the day to go home. Frustration was felt by everyone.

When he arrived home, the bomb squad did another search and declared the home clear. With all that was going on in his head, he wasn't as relieved at the news as he should have been. The squad knew about Rocky and understood.

He showered to remove what he could of the day. His heart ached for Angelina and Taylor. He knew his day could not get any worse.

He was wrong. When the sun went down, it got a whole lot worse.

Chapter

20

Roger's phone rang while he stood in his living room. When he answered, an emotional captain was on the phone.

"Roger? Parry here. I'll make this short. Rocky died on the operating table. Then when he was told his only child had died, his father had a heart attack right there in the hospital and died. Rocky's aunt is taking care of the arrangements. That's it. Can't talk about it now. See you tomorrow." He hung up.

Roger stood in his living room, clutching the phone to his ear. It was after eight in the evening and he wasn't sure what he just heard or if he imagined it. He stood there holding the phone, stunned until the words came back to him.

One. At. A. Time.

Reality set in and he dropped the phone, fell to his knees when the pain overcame him and cried. For a long time, he cried. Rocky, his friend, his partner. Why?

It was over an hour before he was able to get up from the floor. Drained of any emotion, his actions were on auto.

He got ready for bed and laid awake all night staring at the ceiling. He didn't remember having any thoughts at all.

When he got ready for work the next morning, he was still in shock. He was emotionally burnt out and operating on auto. Which was a lot better than the pain he felt the night before.

He wasn't the only one. At the station, everyone was quiet and reserved. Some came over and gave him a pat on the back in sympathy. How quickly bad news spreads.

Staring at his desk top for about two hours, he had not touched a single sheet of paper. He went into Parry's office and said, "I can't…"

"Get out of here. We don't need you today." Parry sounded gruff, but his detectives knew him. He was a tender-hearted sweetheart when it came to his men. His heart was breaking over Rocky, too. Plus he had to worry about losing Roger as well.

Without another word, Roger left and started for home. But home isn't where he wanted to be, at least not alone.

He had to see Angelina and Taylor. He just

261

had to be where there was some kind of happiness. He was reaching for his cell phone when it rang.

"Hi, it's Angelina. How are you doing? I was wondering if you could come over this afternoon. If you have work to do, I will understand and we can do it tonight. What do you think?"

"I'll be right there!" For the first time in days, his smile came back as he turned at the next intersection to head her way.

Upon arriving, Angelina opened the door before he even got on the porch. She was not in her chair. What a nice sight that was.

She put her arms around him and gave him a big hug. He had no problem hugging her back.

Walking into the living room, he was surprised to see Derrick Porter sitting on the couch.

"Whoa. I thought we threw him out days ago." Roger was making a joke to hide his surprise.

Derrick and Angelina laughed.

"Yeah, detective, but it obviously didn't work. I have been here everyday since then!" Derrick had a big grin on his face.

What did that mean? Why has he been here every day? Is he putting the moves on Angelina? I will kil...

"Derrick has been helping me deal with all of the legal aspects of Adriana's estate. You didn't think they were just going to change the name on the title of this house to mine without a court order did you?" Angelina giggled, seemingly unaware of the jealousy in Duncan's heart.

"Yeah, and all of the other legal stuff that needed to be done. Adriana did own half the firm, so that would be Angelina's now." Derrick was not Angelina. He could see the jealousy in the detective's eyes and was amused.

"Anyway, please, everyone, let's go sit at the dining room table so we can sort this out." She led the way.

After all were settled, Angelina nodded at Derrick, so he started.

"Okay, so Adriana owned half the firm. I have paid $1.5 mil to buy her out, which means that money goes to Angelina. And being the smart person she is, she had that entire amount put into a trust for Taylor. Not available at the usual twenty-one years of age, but upon her graduation from college. A brilliant move. Once she has her degree, the money will give her the opportunity to strike out on her own or invest in what interests her the most. "

"I thought about making it later in her life, but I trust Taylor will have enough sense not to waste it." Angelina smiled.

It was Derrick again, "Adriana had approximately nine-hundred-thou in various bank accounts, not including investment holdings. It all was turned over into Angelina's name, as well as the house, cars, and the two rental properties her sister owned. All of which, I might add, are completely paid for. I didn't even know about the rentals. But then again, we all know there was a lot I didn't know about her dealings!"

Everyone laughed at the thought. Adriana was the only one who knew what Adriana was up to.

"So, that's when Angelina wanted me to draw up her will. Of course, being the smart lady that she is," Derrick looked at her fondly, much to Roger's dismay, "she insisted upon first having a psychological test done so no one could later accuse her of not being in her right mind, thus making the will null and void. Man, I wish all of my clients were this intelligent."

Roger was impressed but didn't understand his part in all this legal work. "Okay, so everything has been legally taken care of. I am truly glad to hear it, but why did you want me here?" He was getting irritated at being included in what seemed like a threesome.

Derrick got up and headed for the door. "I have to run an errand, guys. I will be back in a couple hours. Try not to miss me." He went out the door.

Roger was really confused now. *Why did he take off like that? What is going on?*

Looking as beautiful as ever, Angelina said, "Remember when you said you loved me? Well, I haven't forgotten it. I never thought I would hear those words again, at least not from a man.

"The thing about it, Roger, is I love you, too. It all happened so fast but my world revolves around you."

Did Roger hear those words right? He was

staring at her with wide eyes.

"I asked Derrick to leave when we got to this point in our conversation, so I could tell you…"

Roger was out of his chair and had her bent backward in hers while he kissed her on the mouth. After sitting her back up, he got on his knees and continued to kiss and hold her.

Finally, she was laughing while she pushed him away.

"Not that I am not enjoying this very much, but let's finish the legal work first, Detective Roger!"

He slid back into his chair but moved it next to her and smiled at her. He didn't think he had ever been this happy in his life. No, he *knew* he had never been this happy in his life!

"So," Angelina started, "the reason I told you, I didn't think it was a good idea for you to adopt Taylor? Well, you know the system,

Roger! A single man, who works some sixteen hour days and carries a gun, come on. You wouldn't stand a chance. I can't leave Taylor's life just to chance. I know you would be a perfect father for her and I know she is so attached to you. There is a better way."

"My will leaves everything I have to you upon my death… after we are married. You see, if we are married, no one will even question that Taylor is your child. Before I leave, though, I want you to adopt her legally so she can carry your name. You are the only father figure she knows. What do you think?"

"You want to *marry* me? You *really* want to marry me? You will marry *me*? You *will?*" The thought of marriage was not the misery it normally was. It was…well, awesome! She wanted to marry *him!*

"Uh, earth to Roger…!" She laughed as she watched his stunned look.

"I want to marry you if you want to marry

me. How's that?" Angelina put it as straight forward as she could.

He got down on one knee beside her chair and took her hand.

"Angelina, would you do me the honor of being my wife?"

"Yes. Yes, I will."

For the next half hour, they hugged and kissed. He told her over and over he loved her.

"Roger, there are a couple of things I want to ask of you."

"Anything. I will do anything…"

"I want you to raise Taylor here in this house. I know you own your own…"

"I don't care. Whatever you want!" That house didn't matter. He was talking about his family here! His *family!*

She grinned. "Okay, and I want you to make sure she knows which one of the twins was her mother. I don't want her life ruined by Adriana's actions."

"Not a problem, my darling, sweet, wonderful, wife-to-be. I would never let her forget what a fabulous mother she had."

"Hey, you haven't even asked *when* we are getting married! I don't have forever, you know?"

"Uh, yeah, whenever you want to! How about yesterday?"

"Can't. I'm busy yesterday. But, what are you doing a week from Saturday?"

Chapter

21

"Weekend after this one? Get married in a little more than a week?" Roger was ecstatic and shocked at the same time.

"Hello, anyone home?" Derrick came charging through the front door, grinning. He knew the truth would have been told to Roger by now so there would be no more jealousy.

"Come on in, Derrick." Angelina smiled at

him as he walked into the dining room. Roger was still staring at her about their wedding day.

Laughing at Roger's shocked look, Derrick couldn't help but say, "Well, I see you told him about his wedding day! I have what you sent me out to get!" he handed a plastic sack to Angelina.

Roger looked up at him and slowly smiled. Derrick put out his right hand to shake his.

"Congrats, my friend. I don't have a clue what she sees in you, but you are one lucky man. I would have run off with her myself, but you are all she could talk about until I was bored out of my mind!"

Roger returned to holding her hand and had to remind himself this was not a dream and his heart had not made this up. Then suddenly it dawned on him, Taylor wasn't there.

"Where's Taylor? I haven't seen Taylor?"

"She's at the park with Carol. I knew we

would want some alone time. They will be back in about an hour if you want to wait."

"My darling, Angelina, you couldn't drive me away."

Roger couldn't believe what a few hours had done. Yesterday was one of the worst of his life, losing a good friend and partner. Today was definitely the best of his life, knowing he would get to marry Angelina, and adopt Taylor.

The three of them spent the next hour discussing how this marriage was to take place. Derrick produced the marriage license for him to sign. Angelina already had. He said he would file it in the morning, so it would be on record. His judge friend who had helped him escalate the estate issues for Angelina, said he would be happy to perform the ceremony right here in their home.

Roger's phone rang, interrupting the happy conversation. Seeing the number, he excused himself, left the room and answered.

"Yo, man, I found who wants you dead. I am trying to track him now, but I will have more info for you. Just give me a few days more. Just wanted you to know, bro, I have your back."

Roger thanked Roberto and hung up. He stood there for a few moments taking everything in. Good news just keeps coming in.

Once he returned to the conversation, Angelina told him the wedding would be at three o'clock, a week from Saturday, out back by the pool.

She had already opened the package Derrick picked up for her and handed one small box to Roger. It was a gold wedding band. She had a small box as well with an identical band for herself. Ironically, Rogers fit him perfectly, but hers was a little bit loose. She laughed and said she had just enough time to get it sized before the big event.

The wedding would be catered, she informed them, and it was already taken care of.

At that, Roger, trying to appear serious, said, "Boy, you sure were certain I would say *yes*, weren't you?"

"Of course. What choice did you have? It's the wedding or the hole I dug out behind the garage!"

Roger pretended to be in fear for his life and said, "Uh, yeah, I would be glad to get married… I think."

The three laughed until the tears came.

The joking continued with Roger asking Derrick, "You *sure* you don't want to run off with her?"

"Aw, no man, I think I'm busy that year! Besides, that hole was dug for a tall guy like you!"

Roger called Lou and asked him to be his best man. He told his good friend he could bring his mother, partner, neighbor, anyone he wanted to. Laughter was shared. Lou said he didn't think it would be a problem since he and Donna had a gazillion days of vacation coming.

Angelina got on the phone and asked Lou if his partner, Donna, would mind being her maid of honor since she didn't know many people. Lou said he would check it out and let her know.

Derrick asked if he could be with Taylor as ring bearer and Roger thought that was a great idea.

When Taylor and Carol came home there was a lot of excitement. After things settled down, Angelina told the little girl of the upcoming nuptials. Carol was more shocked than Taylor.

"Is he going to be my daddy?" She had leaned over to her mother and whispered in a loud voice.

"I don't know, honey. Do you want him to be?" Angelina could see the worried look on

Roger's face. She knew Taylor didn't remember her real father and she longed for a man to love.

"Yes! He's my daddy. He brought me back to you!"

"Yes, he did, sweetheart. Yes, he did." Roger and Angelina both had watery eyes over that remark.

He picked up the child and held her on his lap. "I would be honored to be your father. I can't think of anything better."

"Daddy!" Taylor threw her arms around his neck and clung for dear life.

Everyone present was touched, but none like Roger, himself, who knew he was holding a piece of Heaven. He didn't even try to stop a tear from falling.

Later, after Taylor was tucked in bed and Derrick left, Carol said she was going to her room to watch TV. Roger and Angelina were able to talk alone.

"I hate to ruin what is possibly one of the happiest days of my life, but I have to tell someone."

"Yesterday, my partner, Rocky Reynolds, was shot in the back and died on the operating table. To make this nightmare even worse, his father, Sam, had a heart attack and died when he was told about it. There will be a double funeral that I have to go to in Oregon, in a few days time."

After she asked, he explained why the funerals would be in Oregon. They both cried over Roger's loss and Angelina asked if he would mind if she went with him.

He couldn't think of anything better.

~~~

After going home that night, he called his captain.

"Well, it's about time I heard from you! Did you think you were going to get married without my knowing about it? Well?"

"Uh, that is why I was calling, captain. I know you are busy and all, but if you could take a little time off to come by…"

"Of course I will be there. JoAnne, too! We wouldn't miss this! The world-renown bachelor is finally getting hitched. I can't believe it. And from what I hear, she's really ugly!"

They both laughed and Roger told him all of the particulars of time and place. Though he didn't ask, Parry told him to take a week off because he would just be useless around there anyway. Roger laughed and agreed.

He then called Lou to talk about his new life. Happiness appears in strange places, but he was ready for it.

Lou agreeing to be Roger's best man, was such an honor for him. But, his heart wanted to ask Rocky.

Chapter

22

The next few days were a blur. Roger spent as much time with Angelina as he could, but so many things needed to be done.

He made plane reservations to go to Oregon for Rocky and his father's funerals. He was not surprised to find out Captain Parry and his wife were on the same plane. After contacting the airline, they arranged for their seats to be together.

Taylor was left in the good care of Carol and they left the day before the services. Roger insisted upon her taking the wheelchair because no one knew when she would get too tired to walk.

"I am feeling fine. I feel stronger each day." Angelina didn't give up without a fight.

"I don't care! I do not want you overdoing it just for my sake." Duncan was not going to lose this one.

Angelina sighed, then smiled and agreed.

Once in Portland, both couples obtained rooms in the same hotel. Roger started to get two rooms, but Angelina insisted upon one.

"Hey, if you snore, it's time for me to find out!" She laughed along with the other three.

That night they slept in the same bed, but Roger did not touch her. He told her he really wanted to wait for their wedding night. Angelina smiled and agreed.

The following day, they rented a car and all went together to the afternoon services.

The local police department gave Rocky a full police honor funeral as if he were their own and died in the line of duty. There was the Casket Watch, where officers have the high honor of protecting the casket during the wake or services. Officers were replaced every 30 minutes to make sure they were rested and ready to protect one of their own, even in death.

After the church services, the drive to the cemetery was accompanied by Police in uniform lining the streets and riding motorcycles.

The grave site was completed by an Honor Guard with seven officers shooting off 3 rounds each for the twenty-one gun salute at the grave site. Hundreds of officers in uniform were present, even though Rocky was not one of their own. Roger was not sorry when he cried. His partner was going to be greatly missed.

Cecil Reynolds and his father, Samuel Reynolds, were buried next to each other, beside his mother. The aunt, the only surviving relative broke down and had to be helped away from the cemetery.

After the services, Captain Parry was pulled aside by his Oregon counterpart to discuss the case.

Roger stayed by the grave site. He couldn't seem to look away.

How could I have lost my partner while he was on vacation? How is that possible? How many jobs did we have reason to fear for our lives, only to die this way? WHY?

Angelina continually held his hand and did not try to interfere with any of his emotions. He was there for her at Adriana's funeral, and she was there for him now.

Late afternoon found them at the aunt's house, along with other mourners. Rocky was everywhere, yet, nowhere. Roger couldn't quite deal with it.

A couple of hours later, they headed for the airport to catch the return flight home. This time, there wasn't much chatter. The silence gave them all the time to deal with what had taken place. Acceptance was the hardest part of losing someone you care deeply for.

Roger was used to seeing him everyday. He knew he would continue to see him everyday for some time to come.

~~~

The morning after their return was filled with activity.

For Roger's part, he hired Boyce's Moving Service to come into his house and pack up all of his personal belongings and move them to the new house. Bob Boyce was happy to hear how things turned out for him and Angelina.

After giving pieces of furniture away to friends, he called the local charity to donate the rest. Last but not least, a cleaning team came in and scrubbed the place from top to bottom, so it could be put up for sale.

Roger couldn't believe it. Two months ago, if someone had told him he would readily sell his house, he would have laughed out loud. There is no way that would happen, yet here he is, happily clearing everything out so he can move on with his life. He was happier than he could ever remember being.

Angelina spent her time preparing the back yard for a fairly large group of people. The more people who heard about it, the more that wanted to come. Her favorite color was blue, so she selected a beautiful soft blue dress for Donna Decker who said she would love to be her Maid of Honor. The best man was supplied with a matching tie and handkerchief to go with his navy suit.

The night before the wedding was a Friday. After all settled down and everyone was gone for the day, Roger and Angelina sat in the living room to finally chat alone.

"I want you to know how much I love you, Roger. After my husband died, I never thought I would ever feel that again, but I do." She spoke softly with a smile.

"You are the only woman I have ever loved, so this is all new to me. I have to say it is wonderful."

"Honey, I hope you are not too upset about my not wanting a honeymoon away from here." Angelina watched for any sign on Roger's face.

He didn't hesitate. "Of course not. Whatever you want is what I want. I can understand you not wanting to be away from Taylor. Quite frankly, I would miss her so much myself, so staying here is perfect for me, too."

He kissed her softly on the lips and said

goodnight. He went upstairs to a guest room and closed the door.

~~~

Saturday was filled with sunshine and laughter. Even though the wedding was not until three in the afternoon, people started arriving at noon.

First, the caterers had to set up the tables and chairs, as well as get the food in place. The florist was bringing in the biggest bouquets Roger had ever seen. A seamstress made the final touches to the white wedding dress Angelina would be wearing. Last, but not least, his Tux arrived, altered and ready for him to wear.

When the band arrived, all of the instruments had to be precisely put where needed. Roger had never seen such a showcase of people in his life. He would never underestimate the preparation for a wedding again.

Guests started arriving at two o'clock. By the time the service started, the large back yard was filled to capacity with folding chairs. There had to be one hundred people. The yard had become a park.

The groom wore the tuxedo his future bride insisted upon buying him. Roger, along with Lou and Donna were all in place, waiting for the big moment to begin.

When the clock struck three, the live band started "Here Comes The Bride." Everyone stood and when they turned to watch, Angelina was walking to the podium escorted by Captain George Parry.

Roger was surprised because no one had told him she wanted the captain to give her away. Roger felt bad because it never occurred to him that she would need someone to walk her down the aisle.

Behind his bride, came Derrick, holding hands with Taylor, who held a pillow with the rings on it. He looked as happy as the groom did.

The audience was quiet as the judge explained the sovereignty of the marriage vows. The ceremony was blessed with love and over too quickly.

After both said 'I do,' the crowd stood and cheered while Roger and Angelina just looked at each other with tears in their eyes.

"I love you, shorty."

"I love you, too, tall person."

When he was sure the day couldn't be more perfect, things even got better. There was a surprise waiting for Roger.

The judge who married them raised his voice and said, "Ladies and Gentlemen! May I have your attention, please! Please be seated. We have one more matter to take care of before we can celebrate this incredible union.

"Mr. Porter, would you please bring Taylor

to the front."

Derrick walked Taylor up to the front. He then picked her up and handed her to Roger. Not a sound could be heard from the guests as they tried to figure out what was going on. Roger, himself, didn't know.

The judge started up again.

"According to Roger and Angelina's wishes, I will now sign into law the adoption of Taylor by Roger Duncan, who is now her legal father!

"I now give you Roger and Angelina Duncan with their daughter, Taylor Duncan!" He then signed the paper in front of him and handed it over to Derrick to file on Monday.

Firecrackers went off all around the yard and the guests went nuts. The cheering could be heard for blocks.

Roger held Taylor close and let a couple of tears fall. Lou and Donna were all over them with congratulations and love. Angelina cried as Taylor hugged her daddy's neck. They were now a family. The Duncan's, at your service.

The afternoon was spent partying and dancing. Some came prepared to swim in the pool. It was after ten that evening when all the guests finally made it to their cars.

Lou, Donna, Parry and his wife, JoAnne, were the only ones left.

"You really surprised me when I saw you walking Angelina! Why didn't you guys tell me?"

Angelina said, "Because I wanted it to be a surprise."

"I only did it because she's so ugly!" With that JoAnne punched his arm and led him out the door.

Lou and Donna sat for a few moments to express their happiness for them.

"Angelina, you are the only one in the whole world that could get this man's heart. Boy, I am sure glad you came along when you did. He was getting old and cranky!" It was Lou poking fun.

The joking continued for a few moments before they, too, left the new couple alone.

Their room had been moved to the upstairs master with Taylor in her own room. Angelina was able to climb the long stairway that evening, but the following week, a company was coming in to install an elevator to reach from the basement up to the second floor.

After quietly and gently making love, Roger held his wife as they whispered their hopes for the future.

They were in the same position when they woke the next morning.

Chapter

23

Captain Parry insisted he take another week off to be with his new family since he had months of vacation piled up. Roger was grateful for the offer.

They spent the days with Taylor, who was starting to learn to read. They went to parks in the afternoons or would sit out by the pool. They took day trips around Kansas to show Taylor things she had never seen.

The nights were spent in each other's arms. Sometimes it was to make love, and others just to hold each other close.

While he was home, the new elevator was installed. Being added where the winding staircase curved, you couldn't tell it wasn't there when the house was built. What a convenience. So far, Angelina insisted upon walking up the stairs. But it gave Roger satisfaction knowing it was there whenever she might need it.

The days flew by but were memories he knew he would take to his grave. God had been so good to him.

Another bar-b-q was held for all his friends on the last weekend before he had to return to work. Everyone was happy and loved teasing him about finally getting "caught."

Angelina would jump right in agreeing with them. He was hers and there was nothing he could do about it. She kept the 'hole behind the garage' threat going if he ever decided to leave.

If he joked back, she would point to the back side of the garage, and everyone would lose it.

"See? See what I have to live with? I have to do everything she says or it will be the end of me. I sleep with one eye open!"

After the week was over, Roger knew it was time to get back to work. The captain had been generous with allowing him so much time off. But with Rocky not there any longer, the captain was short two detectives. That couldn't be easy on him.

The insurance company had settled on his car and he added enough money to buy a new black Expedition. He was happy to get rid of the fleet car and refused to drive Angelina's Mercedes. After all, that was her car. Her old one had been donated to charity.

On Monday morning he kissed her goodbye and gave Taylor a big hug as he walked out the door. Driving to work, his phone rang. It was his real estate agent. He had received a full offer on his house and they needed to know if he would accept a two-week closing. He agreed and was thrilled. Could things get any better?

The first day back was filled with good feelings and congratulations from his co-workers. During the morning, he would look at the ring on his finger and marvel at how good he felt.

What he wasn't taking into consideration was the fact that what goes up, must also come down.

"Duncan. In my office."

Thinking he was going to get a new assignment, he sat in the chair at Parry's desk.

"I didn't want to ruin the time you had with your new wife, Roger, but there is something we need to talk about."

That didn't bode well and Roger sat straight up, wondering what was going on.

"At Rocky's funeral, I spoke with the captain there, as you know. Well, after he was shot and the paramedics loaded him into the ambulance to take him to the hospital, Sam got into the car to follow them. That's when he found a Sunflower laying on the driver's seat."

"He...*WHA*..."

"Just listen for a moment. Sam didn't think anything about it, just the usual curiosity of not having seen it before, plus his mind was on much more serious things at that time. He moved it to the other side, got in and drove away.

"He was able to speak to Rocky for just a moment before he went into surgery. Rocky told him he didn't know anything about the Sunflower. That is when Sam told the police, and they retrieved it from their vehicle.

"Now, I don't have to tell you what I'm thinking. With a Sunflower found next to Adriana's body, the pieces by your car and now this..."

Roger's mind was dancing all directions. "It can't be the same person! We are talking about 1,800 miles away! How could that be? It doesn't make any sense!"

"Don't forget, Roger, Rocky lived here. The police in Portland are convinced it was not random, that he was targeted. I am afraid I have to agree. I think someone went to Oregon to kill him since that is where he was at the time, but Rocky would have killed here if he had not left."

"To my knowledge, captain, Rocky and Adriana had never even met each other. What could possibly be the connection between them." Roger hurt inside. His partner was targeted? And he has a target on himself.

"I don't know yet, but you need to check into it, and fast. We don't know who this guy will target next. But, you were right about one thing. He is the Sunflower Killer. Whoever is after *you* is the same guy who killed Adriana and Rocky.

"Check all your past cases. Someone who would want both of you dead. So far, they have accomplished half the task. Roger, I don't want to lose two detectives."

"Uh, no, I don't want you to, either! I haven't even given it any thought since I got married. So you think both Rocky and I have been targeted by the same person? And how does Adriana fit into any of this?"

"No clue. Collateral damage, maybe." Parry waved him off to get back to work.

Roger went back to his desk and spent the afternoon researching any possible connection between the two. Did Rocky ever need her legal expertize? Did he ever frequent the same places? Nothing was making sense.

He also went back through some of his past cases. Was there someone who might have been paroled and was looking for revenge? Sure. No one likes to be sent to prison. But was there anyone who didn't care if they were sent back for killing a police detective? Or two?

By the end of the day, he was mentally exhausted. Once he arrived at home, his happiness returned as he sat at dinner with his wife and daughter.

That night when they lay in bed, Angelina told him she had four calls that day, but when she answered they hung up. That threw Roger into thinking about all of the calls he kept getting the same way.

Fear filled him. Someone wanted him dead and knew his home phone number, one that he had only obtained a week before!

He certainly didn't want Adriana's old phone number so they had it changed when they married. Roger, himself, couldn't remember it half the time. He had to write it down, at least for now.

~~~

The following morning, at the captain's request, he moved all of the folders and information into the captain's office. They each scoured everything, going over every step, every call, every person, hoping for some sort of resolution in this case.

For the first time, he also brought up the hang-up calls for both his cell and his new home phone. After Angelina told him she was getting the same calls, he now believed they had to be connected. But how did the person find out what the new phone number was at his place of residence?

From the first break-in at his house to the bombing of his car, then add the price on his head, Roger was sure whoever killed Rocky was after him. The only thing they knew at this time was it was not one of the gangs.

"Have you heard from your informant? I thought he was supposed to have answers for you."

Roger told Parry he hadn't heard from Roberto for about two weeks. That was odd, because he said he would get back in a couple of days, but that never happened. Surely something didn't happen to him, too?

While he was still with the captain, he called Roberto but got his voice mail. He left a message to call him right away.

It was near eleven when his cell rang. It was not Roberto. It was Angelina.

"Roger. You need to come home. Right now."

He was immediately on edge. She normally addressed him with the more endearing terms such as honey or darling. He got the captain's attention, then answered.

"What's wrong honey. Why should I come home right now?"

"Just do it." She hung up.

Roger was in a panic and Parry told him to get home.

He flew down the streets and didn't even remember the drive to Eastborough. His mind was cluttered with thoughts of what could possibly be happening to his beloved wife.

Roger pulled into the driveway and ran for the front door. Once inside, his heart stopped.

Angelina had a gun to her head.

Chapter

24

"WHAT THE…!" Roger could see nothing but the fear on his new wife's face.

Holding her around the neck from behind, with a gun pointed to her head, was Kristina, his ex-girlfriend.

"Well, hello Roger! Aren't you going to say it's nice to see me again? No? Well, that's too bad. Don't even think about reaching for your gun, darling. She won't last a second."

"Kristina! What are you doing? Put that gun down! Let her go. What is wrong with you?"

"What is wrong with me? Why, don't you remember, darling, you dumped me. Yes, that's right. I loved you and you dumped me like I was trash. Did you really think you would get away with that? Did you really think I wouldn't make you pay for your evil deeds?" Kristina was beyond angry and with every thought of his misdeeds, she held tighter to Angelina.

"But, you found another man to love and you are engaged to be married to him! What about the doctor?"

"What about him? Of course, we will be married. But that will come after I settle the score here. You know, after you and your little wife pay for breaking my heart.

Roger was shocked. "Kristina, I thought you agreed to the parting. We talked about it. I didn't know of any hard feelings. I am sorry if I hurt you!"

"You are sorry? *Sorry?* Oh, you will be sorry all right. You didn't pay any attention to any of my other warning signs, but you won't be able to miss the death of your new bride, now will you?"

"Kristina, don't! What other warning signs? Were you the one that broke into my house and painted on my wall? Was that you? But you didn't have the code to my alarm or a key to the house." Roger was searching his brain for answers.

"As always, you underestimated me. It was easy to get another key made. You kept a spare on a hook in the kitchen. I just took it one day. Since you didn't need the spare, you didn't even notice it was gone. Of course, I had a key made for me. Something you should have done long before. The next time I was over, I returned the spare.

"And that alarm code? Really, Roger? How

309

many times did you set it or unset it when I was right there with you? How stupid are you? Like I said, all you ever did was underestimate me.

"I put the money up for your death, which was actually put up by you, but you know that. I thought you had money in that house, but it took a little while to find it. Of course, trashing the place that you were so fond of was the highlight of my day.

"Unfortunately, I couldn't get any idiot to kill you. Seems killing a cop is different than killing someone else. Well, not to me."

Roger sat down on the couch as he raced to put the pieces together.

"The bombing of my car?"

"Of course that was me. You were supposed to be in it, you two-timing scumbag!"

"Two-timing? I never cheated on you?"

"And just what do you call that arrogant

310

attorney you were with? It was obvious she thought you belonged to her. I came over to this very house and tried to explain to her you were mine, for her to leave you alone.

"I even offered her a beautiful Sunflower as a token of my sincerity. Sunflowers are my favorite flower in the whole world, but you didn't know that, did you, dear? You never wanted to know anything about what I liked. But then again, you never bought me flowers either.

"Do you know what that egotistical witch did? She laughed at me. She *laughed* at me! She said no man would want someone as sorry as I was and the flower was even more stupid! Then she turned her back on me. She turned away from me like I wasn't worth her time. Well, I showed her, didn't I? I showed her who the winner really was."

"YOU killed Adriana?"

"What did I just say? No woman in her right mind is going to allow the competition to win!"

311

Kristina turned her head and looked into the dining room.

Roger followed her look and found two large sunflowers laying on the dining room table. He choked as he continued, "Oh my God. You. You are the one who killed Rocky. You killed my partner, Rocky!"

"Well, stupid, I wasn't able to get your attention any other way, and I kept missing you, so I figured you would see that coming back to me was better than ending up like him, but no. You weren't bright enough to put it together. I would have dumped the doctor in a heartbeat if you had wanted me back, but no. Sometimes I wonder what I ever saw in you.

"Do you have any idea how I felt after sending all these messages to you and then I see your wedding announcement in the newspaper? *You? Getting married?* I couldn't believe it. You wouldn't even let me live in the same house with you, and you were going to marry a woman you just met a few weeks ago? That was it, Roger. That was the straw. I called it the Sunflower straw. Don't you think that's cute? No?

"I had to find out what this woman had that I didn't have. And you know what? She has nothing! She doesn't even have any hair? I know she looks like her sister, but really, Roger. Is that the only way you could keep Adriana around?"

"Adriana and I were not dating, Kristina. I was investigating her in a kidnapping." He wanted to add 'now who's the idiot,' but didn't want to push her over the edge.

"You know what, Roger? I have to admit I was going to give you another chance. If you would just forget marrying this newbie and come back to me, I would have forgiven you.

"I drove over to your house to talk to you about it and I got the shock of a lifetime. There was a For Sale sign in the yard and a Sold sign over it. The house you thought more of than me, you actually sold, apparently for this loser. I have to say, Roger boy, I was shocked. Did you really think I would not know how to find you?"

During this entire conversation, Angelina was keeping quiet and watching her husband. She was casually dressed with a scarf around her head. She didn't wear a wig when Roger wasn't home. She knew he was sneaking looks at her when he could.

He was also very aware of where his gun was but was not about to reach for it. Angelina would be dead before he could touch it.

"Kristina, let's set down and talk about this. You don't have to do anymore harm…"

"Shut up, you pig. I know *exactly* what I have to do. You get to watch this loser die and then it will be your turn. No one treats me like you did."

Even though he was in total concentration of every move Kristina made, he heard shuffling from outside somewhere. When he realized what it was, panic filled his heart. Carol and Taylor came home and was entering the back door.

"Daddy, you're home! Where are you!"

In total surprise, Kristina swung her head around to look behind her at the noise.

Taylor! She will kill Taylor! Roger took the one last chance he had to save his family. Drawing his gun he aimed, just as Kristina turned back to him with fury in her eyes, as she screamed *"Daddy? Wha...?"*

He fired.

For the next five seconds or so, she stood there. Angelina wrenched away from her grasp and ran to Roger. They watched as Kristina started to slowly fall. It was in slow motion, but fall she did. The bullet between her surprised eyes did its job.

"Daddy!" Taylor ran through the kitchen into the living room, toward her parents.

Angelina grabbed Taylor and ran from the room to keep her from seeing the dead woman. Carol followed them.

Roger walked over to the body on the floor and just stared. He heard the sirens in the background but didn't have any idea who they were. Within a minute, the house was surrounded by police squads.

Roger didn't care. He got down on one knee beside the woman he just shot and stared at her.

Kristina. I would never have thought it was you. I thought you were happy. I wanted you to be happy...

Before he knew it police were all over the house, including Captain Parry, who tapped him on the shoulder and helped him get up.

"After you left the station, Roberto called me. He said he had tried to call you but got no answer."

Roger realized he was in such a hurry to get into the house, he left his phone in the car.

His boss continued, "He told me he found out who it was. When he told me it was Kristina Peterson, I knew why you were called home suddenly. We got here as fast as we could, but I see you took care of the problem yourself. Good work, detective."

Roger wasn't thinking about much at this point, he only wanted to put his arms around Angelina.

When he turned around, there she was, waiting for him. They grabbed each other and hung on for dear life.

Carol was instructed to play with Taylor in the main floor master while an officer took statements from Roger and Angelina.

"The doorbell rang. I wasn't expecting anyone, but there wasn't any reason for alarm, so I opened the door. She charged in and grabbed me around the neck. Unfortunately, it was not hard to do because she was taller than I am."

Roger was holding her hand all the time she spoke. They were sitting on the living room couch while being interviewed. The coroner's crew was loading up the body and they both tried not to look at her.

"She ordered me to call and get Roger home. I refused at first, but she made it clear she would kill me and then my kid, as she put it, if I didn't. Carol had wanted to take Taylor to the park for a while and I was tickled to have some alone time." Angelina, rubbed her face trying to make sense of it all.

"So I called. She knew he would rush home, so we just stood in the living room and waited. Roger did come home and ran in the front door, just as she planned. She said she killed my sister." Angelina began to weep softly.

When Roger put his arm around her, she looked up at him with a faint smile. "I'm okay.

Just tired, I guess."

It took about two hours for the area to be cleared and the police were all gone. Captain Parry was the last to leave.

"Take the rest of the day off, detective. And tomorrow, too. Your family needs you right now." No one could ask for a better boss. No one.

After the house was empty, Roger had a remediation team come in and clean the carpet. He knew blood was considered a bio-hazard and it needed to be dealt with immediately. Being fresh, all of it came out, but the memory was still there.

Carol disposed of the sunflowers. And after the remediation crew left, they had dinner on the patio, insisting that Carol join them They talked and laughed and felt like a family again.

Roger didn't know how long it would take to register all of the evil things Kristina had done, but he was going to work at getting it out of his mind for good.

That night in bed, it was quiet as Angelina laid in his arms.

"I know the carpet is clean, but I was never crazy about that color in the living room. Wanna go shopping with me this weekend to find something better?"

Roger couldn't believe the wife he married. He laughed and said he would love to.

As long as it wasn't red.

Chapter

25

It had been a month since the tragic event at their home.

It required a massive amount of paperwork to finish the reports on the murders of Cecil Reynolds, Adriana Mason, as well as the multiple attempts at killing Detective Roger Duncan. There was also the attack on the poor man who was hit when Roger's car bomb went off.

Roger was congratulated numerous times for his "taking out" the killer, but he didn't like to be reminded of that time.

The story ran on page one of the paper and made the nightly news for several days. Roger was the hero of the city. He really hated publicity and this was no different.

With the attempt on the life of his wife, her picture was also featured. She couldn't have looked more beautiful. Her sister's crimes weren't left out of the news either, along with the irony of why she was killed.

There were some reporters who had to compare her with Adriana as their readership was mesmerized by the identical twins story. Angelina took it fairly well, knowing it wouldn't last long, but she was grateful Taylor was too young to remember the tragedy which occurred during her early childhood.

There was one who didn't fare as well with the publicity. In all of the humiliation, Dr.

Weston quit his job at Wesley Hospital. He returned to Topeka where he grew up, to set up his own practice and get away from the memory of Kristina.

Roger figured it would be quite a while before he trusted a female again. He couldn't blame him. Kristina had fooled them both.

Part of Roger's mind was not able to believe she was capable of murder. The woman threatening to kill him and his wife was not the woman he dated. Was it? Were there signs he ignored? Was he so blind in his personal life that people could die without him having a clue? He certainly sympathized with the good doctor.

He knew it would take time to internally deal with it all, but one thing he promised himself. He wasn't going to let it dampen one moment with his wife and child.

Angelina was still holding her own and seemed healthy. He could hope, anyway. She looked well and constantly told him she felt great. They knew the cancer was still there, but she was able to enjoy life more than she had in the eighteen months since she was diagnosed. They both were grateful.

The carpet in the living room had been changed to a color they both picked. Roger had to admit, the new one did look better.

It was now Saturday and tonight they were having a long-awaited bar-b-q and everyone was invited. Roger expected about twenty plus people to show up. That would definitely keep him busy at the grill.

Although not asked to, everyone brought a dish of their own and they had a lot of food. Mostly desserts. He was pretty sure he had gained ten pounds just looking at them all.

"Where's the steak and potatoes?"

Roger looked up to see Bob Boyce and his wife come out the French doors into the back yard. He smiled and waved them over.

"Over here! All you can eat! And I am not a half bad cook if I say so myself!"

He gave Bob a welcome hug and met his wife. Everyone was open to bringing anyone they wanted so Bob brought his mother-in-law, Blanche. Roger was glad to see them and started filling their plates.

Lou and his mother, Darlene, made it. Donna Decker brought her parents, and George Parry came with JoAnne. The captain would never miss a free meal so it was pretty certain he would show.

A few of the detectives he worked with came either on their way to work or after they got off. Roger was thrilled they took the time out of their busy schedules to come visit, even for a few moments. He knew how hectic it can be on days they were on duty.

Derrick Porter showed up with a beautiful lady on his arm, Tracy Andrews. They brought Tracy's sister Caroline Wilkerson. Seems

Caroline and Tracy live in a house together just two blocks away in Eastborough. Caroline brought her daughter, Carson, who was four years old. Taylor was overjoyed to have a new playmate and they both headed for the swing-set and mini playground in the back yard.

Derrick said he met his lovely date the year before when he was hired by her sister to defend Tracy, but it turned out to not be necessary since the D.A. determined she had done nothing wrong.

Lana Carter, the private investigator came at Donna's invitation. Her husband, Jim Carter, was with her. Both outgoing people, they kept the jokes and laughter going almost by themselves. Lana also got a chance to meet some of the detectives she didn't know.

Soft music came from a boom-box, and a makeshift bar kept their guests in refreshments.

After everyone had eaten more than they should have, it became quiet around the pool.

Some of the guests were swimming, while others rested in chairs. The cool breeze made the early evening perfect.

Roger couldn't believe how blessed he was.

After fifteen or twenty minutes of peaceful silence, Captain Parry spoke up.

"When you get back to work on Monday, Roger, I have a case with a missing boy...."

Before he could say another word, a pillow hit him in the face.

Epilogue

Life went on for the Duncan's. Angelina lived another five years. Some down times, but mostly good. The doctors didn't know why, but Roger did. It was love, pure and simple, that kept her alive so long. Love she had for him and his love for her.

With Angelina to be with, Roger never played computer chess again. He said all he needed was his family.

She didn't have any more chemo, as the

doctor didn't feel it would do her any good. She would have refused anyway. Chemo did such horrible things to the human body and she said she would never go through it again.

Six months later, they had another big bar-b-q party to celebrate Angelina's own hair growing back. It was the dead of winter for Wichita, but the same crowd all showed up again, wearing coats this time.

The cheers went up when she threw the wig into the fire-pit. After a filling meal, they all gathered inside in the media room to watch a movie. Everyone loved going to the Duncan's home.

Taylor did indeed learn to read by the time she was four and a half. She could also write before she started school. The child became a voracious reader and it was all Roger could do to keep her in books.

They turned a spare bedroom into a library just for her. Walls were ceiling to floor shelves to hold her books. In the center of the room were two love seats facing each other with a table in the center. If you didn't know where she was, you could bet that was the room she would be found in. She had hundreds of ebooks, too, but she preferred those she could hold in her hand.

Darlene McGregor finally said she would dump her son and adopt Roger if Taylor could be her grandchild. Lou begged for another chance, but it remains to be seen if that plea will work.

She did get to babysit Taylor a lot when Lou, Donna, Roger and Angelina all went out together to have fun. Sometimes, Darlene wouldn't let them pick her up until the next day, after Taylor's latest swimming lesson. Seems the child was a natural in water.

Taylor had just turned nine when she lost her mother. It was hard on them both but Roger made it his life's desire to make sure she remembered the wonderful woman Angelina was.

She told her father she wanted to be a writer when she grew up. He knew it was inbred in her. Why else would a three-year-old want to learn to read and write? He was sure she would be excellent at anything she did.

By this time, all talk and headlines about Adriana were long gone, so Taylor never had to deal with her mother's lookalike. All in all, thirty-two people were prosecuted due to their contributing to Adriana's illegal actions.

Roger went onto become a top detective, winning an award for meritorious service. Detective Jim Palmer was eventually assigned to be his new partner and they worked well together.

Derrick Porter went on to marry Tracy, the lady he was dating. In their second year of marriage, Tracy gave him twin girls, Diana and Donna.

His friendship with Derrick only deepened with time and he was the only attorney Roger would even think of using in his personal life.

Once Duncan made it known he wholeheartedly recommended Porter & Associates, LLC, business skyrocketed. The last Duncan knew, he had six other attorneys working for him.

The two remained fast friends and often joked about how they met. One thing Roger would never let him forget was his passing out at the sight of Angelina. Derrick was going to have to live with that for the rest of his life.

When Angelina passed away, Carol retired to her little house and a new person had to be hired. Taylor was happy with her new nanny, but she would call Carol from time to time to see how she was doing.

And Roger?

Roger was so happy with the five years the Lord allowed him to have with Angelina, to say nothing of the precious daughter he was given.

He knew in his heart that Angelina would not have survived two months if they hadn't met. God had given them *both* a miracle.

Each other.

Thank you for reading THE SUNFLOWER
KILLER. I hope you enjoyed it as much as I did
writing the story.

I would appreciate it if you would go to
Amazon.com, type in my name, select your title,
then leave a review.

It will only take a moment of your time and
it means so much to an author to hear from her
readers.

God Bless,

Donalie Beltran

www.ingramcontent.com/pod-product-compliance
Lightning Source LLC
Chambersburg PA
CBHW062013170626
46813CB00001B/140